HIMALAYAN HEIST

IRIS LEIGH

Contents

Thank you to my best friend Amy,
For if it wasn't for you I wouldn't have become a cat aunt to
three amazing but annoying cats who inspired this story.

Himalayan Heist Blurb

They say diamonds are a girl's best friend, but in my world, jewelry is a cat's best friend.

I like many things, but talking cats isn't one of them. *Especially talking cats.* Not even the Himalayan cat who thinks I'm for hire.

Some might call me delusional. Others might say I'm eccentric. Whatever the case, I'm not interested. Nothing will make me change my mind... until the home I'm housesitting is burglarized.

I can't just walk away. Despite my reluctance, I must work with the cats to find the burglar and retrieve the missing jewelry. But for the record, I'm still not working for the cats... *I swear.*

Chapter One

The breeze was slightly chilly as it brushed against me. With only a thin jacket to block against the wind, it wasn't much, but luckily it wasn't freezing. My hands dug even deeper into the pockets of my pants as I continued my stroll down the street toward the café. People passed by but they were all too busy on their phones or talking to their companions to notice my approach.

"Hi."

"Hi."

I instantly responded, despite not being sure who was talking or if they were even addressing me. But if someone said hi in passing on the street, it didn't hurt to acknowledge it. It might make somebody's day.

"Are you Kat Jones?"

Now that was weird. My progress halted as I looked about, trying to identify who was talking to me. As I scanned the people around me, no one was looking my way, and no one had stopped walking. Everyone was continuing with their business. With one last look about to make sure I wasn't crazy, I walked forward again. But I soon paused as a thought popped into my head.

It couldn't be, but it technically could ...

I could still talk to cats, but surely there wouldn't be a cat talking to me in public? I hoped that wasn't the case as I tried to swallow the lump in my throat that had formed from the crazy thought of a cat talking to me in public. A quick brushing sensation against my legs caused me to look down and into the blue eyes of a mostly white cat with brown fur around its face.

"Hi." It spoke again.

However, I would not respond to a cat, especially not out in public. That was what crazy people did, and I wasn't crazy. Nope, that wasn't me at all. Instead of continuing my walk down the street, I broke into a light jog as I tried to put distance between me and the cat. It wasn't full-on running because that would draw too much attention. I let out a slew of curses under my breath as I got a quick look behind me to see if the cat was following me. And unfortunately, it was.

"Go away!" I hissed, trying my best to keep my voice low but also loud enough the cat could hear me. I wasn't trying to draw the attention of the passing two-legged folks—I just wanted the four-legged one gone.

"But I hired you!"

"It isn't possible to be hired by a cat!"

This cat was crazy, and it was doing its best to make me out to be nuts as well. Why would a cat think they could hire me? I had never laid eyes upon this cat before, and I would definitely remember if I'd offered my services to a cat, which I had not.

"I already paid for your help to look into a robbery."

My feet skidded to a halt as I whirled on the cat, who had no choice but to stop in its tracks or run into me. My eyes narrowed as I stared down at the cat at my feet, and I crossed my arms over my chest. I did my best to seem menacing, but most likely I was failing. Most people wouldn't classify me as a scary-looking person … unless I was hungry. That was a very different story. Regardless, I had to set this cat straight; I was a human who wasn't for hire.

"Paid for my help with what? Fish?"

"No, jewels."

I scoffed at the cat's words, and a laugh soon erupted. Jewels as payment? Now I knew for a fact this cat was a different type of crazy.

"Right. Do you see any jewels on me?" I asked as I brought my wrists in front of the cat's face, showing that they were bare. Next, I touched my neck and ears to also indicate they were bare and void of jewelry. "No, right? You didn't hire me, so leave me alone."

This time I didn't wait for a reply from the weird cat and instead took off in a sprint once more to get to the café. Thankfully, pets weren't allowed in most businesses unless they were a service animal, and there was no way I would claim any type of association with this cat. I would finally be safe from talking cats and be able to enjoy my day. The distance between the café and me was covered rather quickly. A talking cat was certainly a motivator for the increased speed. Without sparing a single glance behind to see if the cat followed, I strolled up to the counter to order a drink.

"One iced coffee, please."

I grabbed my card from my pocket and handed it to the barista behind the counter, who in return swiped it and handed it back. They followed up by sliding my iced coffee across the counter into my waiting hands. It probably would have been better to have a hot drink because of the slight chill outside, but I could never turn down iced coffee.

I let out a satisfied groan as I took a sip of my drink; the caffeine sent small jitters through my body. Now it was time to find my date, Lewis. Where was he? My eyes scanned the café till they were drawn to a hand that waved as it shot up into the air. I waved my hand in reply and hurried over to join Lewis at a table by a window.

"I thought you might have bailed." He motioned to the empty seat and sent a smile my way.

"Was I that late?"

"No."

"Sorry about that."

"No problem at all. Glad you could make it."

I had provided a quick response to his question but found that it was hard to engage in the conversation we were having for my attention was drawn to something outside. A four-legged feline with blue eyes that looked exactly like the cat from before.

"Are you okay?"

My body chilled, and my heart felt like it stopped beating as Lewis looked over his shoulder. He seemed interested in seeing what was dividing my attention.

"Is that your cat?"

"No, just a random cat. Don't pay it any attention."

"Okay." He turned back around to face me.

"How is your business going?"

The smile on Lewis' face grew as he spilled everything about the personal fitness venture he was starting to pursue. He had already landed quite a few clients and was getting his name known in the city as the go-to person if someone wanted to get in shape. I eased back in my chair and let loose a sigh of relief at successfully changing the topic so we didn't have to address the cat still watching from outside. Lewis excitedly kept going on about his business, it was getting easier to ignore the two blue eyes outside. Whenever I got tempted to see if the cat was still there, I would instead just look down at my drink.

"I'm really glad your business is going well!"

"Thanks! I didn't know it would be such a lucrative field."

I nodded my head along to his words while raising my iced coffee to have another sip. I didn't know how much personal fitness instructors made, but obviously it must have been a good amount based on his comment.

"Do you think—" He started but got cut off as there was a light thumping noise on the outside of the glass window.

The blue-eyed cat was now banging its paw against the window, making a scene and not seeming to care that they were being rude and interrupting my date.

"Are you sure you don't know that cat?"

"Absolutely sure."

The cat continued to bang against the window, even though I was giving it my full attention now.

"I hired you!"

The high-pitched voice of the cat barely filtered through the window. I glanced over to Lewis to see if he had heard the cat speak, but he gave no sign that he had. I wasn't sure what sign I was looking for to see if he understood the cat, but he wasn't freaking out.

If someone had heard a cat speaking, they certainly wouldn't be sitting calmly in their seat. Nope, the only crazy person here was me. I slid down in my chair as I slightly grimaced at the cat, who just kept thumping away. I wanted to die from embarrassment. With my elbow resting on the table, I raised my hand and shielded my eyes to block the cat from my view.

"So what were you saying?"

"I don't remember honestly, but I think that cat really likes you."

"That's funny, considering I don't know that cat."

"I don't think we can just ignore the cat," he said as his eyes stayed focused on the cat, who was still not letting up.

"Excuse me for one second. Sorry."

I pushed myself out of my slouched position in the chair with determination to get this settled once and for all. A few people in the café watched as I made my way outside to confront the feline. It was seriously being a mood killer, and it needed to go away.

"Come here!" I hissed out to the cat to grab its attention as soon as I got close enough.

"Finally! I thought my paw was going to fall off."

"Maybe you should have stopped a long time ago, then?" I bit back as my foot tapped against the ground.

"I wouldn't need to be doing this if you did the job I hired you for."

"Again, how many times do I need to say this? A cat can't hire me!"

"But I did."

My eyes rolled before casting my gaze down to look at the feline sitting at my feet. I needed this cat gone as soon as possible before people started asking questions ... if they weren't already asking questions. I let out a sigh. What had I done to deserve this?

"Look, talking to a cat in public is bad for my

image. I will help you solve whatever you supposedly hired me for but just please go away for now."

"Okay."

That was it? The cat turned on its paws and walked down the street, satisfied with my agreement to help solve whatever case they had hired me for. I let out an enormous sigh of relief at finally getting rid of the cat. I made my way back inside the café. Too bad for the feline that I had no intention of actually following through with helping them. I still knew nothing about this cat, so even if I wanted to find it again, I couldn't. It was for the best if we went our separate ways.

I made my way back over to my seat and slid into the chair, doing my best to make it seem like the last few minutes hadn't happened.

"Are you a cat whisperer?" he muttered softly, his eyes wide as he stared at me. Now that was a better name to be called than crazy, so it was a win in my book.

"You could say I am, in a way." I brought my iced coffee to my mouth and took a huge chug to finish it off.

I needed some type of distraction from everything that had just happened. I snorted at the thought that the cat really thought a feline could hire a human, which in turn caused me to release a choked cry as my drink traveled down the wrong pipe. It seemed cats might actually be the death of me one day.

Chapter Two

"How does a cat hire someone?" I spoke as I got to work opening a can of wet cat food in order to feed Luna and Zaira.

Lola was out about doing who knows what cats did when allowed free roam outside so she would be on the hook for finding her own dinner. It was a weird deal I had with that cat. She was allowed to go as she pleased and the only requirement was that she make it back home a few times for when I received a phone call from their mom. It wouldn't do to worry my best friend while she was out of the country and have her thinking I lost her cat. Almost went there, and it wasn't something I wanted to repeat.

"How should I know? Are you almost done?" Irritation laced Luna's words.

Despite this, I didn't hurry and instead rewarded her with an eye roll. I moved at my own speed, and I would eventually finish getting their food ready. It wasn't like she was going to drop dead from hunger anytime soon. With their food plated, I made my way to the trash can to throw away the now empty can.

"You can't feed us first and then clean up?"

"Really, Luna? You act like you never get fed."

"At this rate, who knows if I will actually get fed tonight."

I took a deep breath in, held it, then slowly released it. No one had warned me that having talking cats would be such a pain. It wasn't like I'd heard about anyone else having the ability to talk to cats, but it would have been nice if this ability had come with a user manual.

I set the two bowls of cat food on the ground near their automatic water fountain. Supposedly using this contraption was better than just putting a water bowl out for the cats, according to the internet. But it only served as a reminder that the cats were starting to run this place. Thankfully, Lola wasn't here today.

"I still can't wrap my head around it. Why would a cat think they hired me? Especially me, of all people. Does everyone know I can talk to cats now?"

The four-legged felines next to me provided no response. They were too busy munching away on their wet cat food. Now that they had gotten their dinner, it was time for me to eat mine. A frozen meal of buffalo mac and cheese, already heated to perfection, waited for me on the dining table. A shiver coursed through my body as I took a seat, the smell filling my nose with many delights. It was the perfect comfort meal to end the crazy day.

"It is possible." Luna's soft voice said as she jumped onto the table to sit by my mac and cheese. On instinct, I wrapped my hand around the bowl to scoot it away. That cat seemed to always be hungry, and one could never be too careful, especially when it involved mac and cheese.

"What is possible?"

"Did you already forget your question? Humans."

My eyes squinted at the jab she had just shot my way. I grabbed my fork and took a big scoop of my food before shoving it into my mouth. Cats that talk were really grinding my nerves. A sudden burst of fire erupted on my tongue as the food was extremely hot. But I refused to cough out the food, instead opening my mouth to take deep breaths of air to help cool it off.

"Seriously?"

After the mac and cheese cooled down a little, I finished chewing and swallowed it down.

"Right," I continued. "The question of whether being hired by a cat is possible. Where would that cat have gotten the idea that I was for hire anyways?"

"We don't exactly know what Lola is doing out there."

"Probably gathering an army." I laughed.

After solving the case of Mrs. Higgins and finding Lola in the woods, surrounded by other cats, it wouldn't surprise me if she were becoming their leader.

"Gathering an army for what?" Luna asked.

I shoved more mac and cheese into my mouth and waved my fork around in the air before answering.

"Shouldn't you know the answer to that? You guys are an odd bunch, after all. Whoever heard of talking cats before?"

"I don't think you have the right to call us odd, considering the fact you were the one who just set her mouth on fire."

This time, though, it wasn't the cat who sat on the table that had spoken. Instead, it was Zaira, who sat by my feet now that she finished her meal. Her nose twitched as she stared up at me. It felt like the face of judgment, but I wasn't sure. I couldn't read the facial expressions of a cat.

"When it comes to buffalo mac and cheese, who cares if my mouth is on fire." I retorted as I shoved another bite into my mouth. This time, though, it wasn't as hot, which allowed for easy consumption.

"Are you going to share?"

"Absolutely not." I shot a look over in Luna's direction, whose eyes had trailed to the movement of my fork as I swirled it around in my bowl.

I didn't trust Luna, as I could see her twitch ever so slightly. I had seen those moves before, right before a cat was ready to pounce, and we would have none of that today. Especially since buffalo mac and cheese was involved. With my free hand, I wrapped it around the bowl and bolted from the table into the kitchen while scarfing down the rest of the food.

"Was that really necessary? I didn't plan on taking it."

"I can never be too careful with you," I shot out as my eyes narrowed at the gray cat. "I will be back later. I have to go to Lucy Walker's house since she is out of town."

Not bothering to wait for a reply from either cat, I grabbed my keys off the counter and headed out the front door. It was starting to get a bit scary, and certainly crazy, having to deal with talking cats every day. After the whole thing with Mrs. Hastings and Rusty, I'd immediately taken to the internet to do some research, to see if anyone else had this experience. But the only mention of people being able to communicate with cats referred to either mythical people or those with superpowers in comics. And I was neither of those.

The street was empty as I made my way to Lucy's home, which stuck out like a sore thumb on our block. Her husband was an architect and had redone their entire home a few years back. Now it was the only contemporary-looking house on this block. A white stone path led the way to the modern front door, with three glass panes vertically placed in the dark-stained wood. I let myself into Lucy's home and remembered the first rule of the house was no shoes allowed. So I kicked off my shoes before venturing farther inside, toward the kitchen.

The one reason she needed someone to stop by was to water her plants. Other than that, she didn't need any help because nothing really happened on the block that would cause her to worry about her home. Except for the death of Rose Hastings, but that was just a one-off. We weren't due to have anything else happen for several years, according to the police. They had told us this after coming to take everyone's statements, when Zack Hastings got sent to jail for Rose's murder. It had caused Mrs. Higgins to laugh.

On the kitchen counter were two watering canisters, that would make maneuvering around the house to water easier. The house wasn't huge, thankfully, so getting everything done quickly would be no problem. A few plants were on the dining room table, and several in the living room. The last stop would be the master bedroom, and then I would be all done and ready to go home. A quick and easy housesitting gig.

Upon entering the master bedroom to make my way to water her plants, I couldn't help but stop and gawk at the beauty of the room. Lucy's husband had done a wonderful job at redesigning the home, and the bedroom was definitely the best part of the house. The bedroom was basically two bedrooms put together, so it was the largest room in the house. Quite larger than the common areas, despite those having the most foot traffic.

To the left side from the door was the actual sleeping area, and the rest of the space was more of a lounge area. The first plants that would need to be watered would be the ones on Lucy's side of the bed. As I poured water into the plant on the nightstand, I stared at the chandelier over the bed. It was over the top, and something I would not buy personally, but it was breathtaking.

Most of the plants were now watered, and the last few were in the bathroom. Lucy's bath plants, as I had dubbed them since they lined the rim of the bathtub. As I turned to head to that direction, I suddenly stopped. Their once beautiful French doors in the sitting area that led outside to the garden were no longer functional. The lavish, white-framed doors that had been mostly glass now lay shattered on the ground, which allowed a soft breeze to filter through the large room—something that I had not noticed upon walking into the bedroom. Underneath the shattered pieces of wood and glass were muddy footprints. Someone obviously didn't know the first rule of Lucy Walker's—no shoes allowed in the home.

Whoever had done that either wanted to piss her off or didn't know her well enough. Either way, we were both going to be at the receiving end of her fury once she found out about it. I moved closer to examine the muddy footprints. Someone had clearly walked in from outside and made their way over to the closet.

What was in the closet that had caused someone to ignore the rest of the home and head straight there? I stared at the slightly cracked closet door, wondering if I actually wanted to find out. Lucy had left her car in the driveway to make it seem like someone was home and the house wasn't sitting empty. So someone had to have known she was out of town and they had to have known exactly what they were looking for and where to find it. So the person probably knew Lucy, yet they still ventured inside with shoes on? That was the type of person I didn't want to meet. I inched toward the closet to see what might have captured the burglar's attention. I grasped the doorknob to open the closet. What if the person was still here?

"Hello?" My voice was strained as I spoke.

A tightness formed in my chest as I waited for someone to respond. But would someone respond? If they did, what was I supposed to do, just have a conversation with them? Run out yelling like a wild person? Nothing was ever simple in this town anymore. There were talking cats, a dead neighbor, and now this. I should probably look into finding a new place to move.

With caution thrown to the wind, I pushed the door open and quickly scanned the closet to see if there was someone hiding. That tightness in my chest turned into the feeling of a bomb dropping and exploding inside my ribcage. The jewelry display dresser in the center of the closet had had its glass shattered as well. This was bad. Clothes lay scattered on the floor, but that paled in comparison to the drawers, which had been yanked out and their glass broken. I took everything in. This was just getting worse and worse.

I slowly made my way to the broken drawers, being careful to not step on anything that might cut my feet. Which would be something I didn't have to worry about if I could wear shoes. I peered down at the top piece of the dresser that acted as a display case. The sunglass holders were present, but all of them were missing their primary purpose for being there, as there were no glasses in sight. Surely someone didn't steal everything in here, right?

I felt extremely sick as I opened the top drawer. All the padding was there to hold jewelry, but there wasn't a single piece in sight. My body hunched over and I could not process everything that was happening. Did I just have the worst luck in the world?

"It can't be that bad ..." I whispered as I tried to calm my pounding heart. But I knew it was a lie. It was bad the second I'd noticed the broken doors. I already knew I was doomed as I opened the last drawers of the dresser, and just like before they were empty.

"Of course there isn't anything left. What was I thinking?"

The person just had to rob Lucy Walker. They

couldn't do us the decency of robbing the Higgins home? At least there I wouldn't have to do anything because Mr. Higgins would handle it. I wasn't sure who had done this, but whoever had was now my least favorite person, for Lucy Walker was going to kill me when she found about all of this.

Chapter Three

The next morning could not come fast enough after what had happened the night before. I didn't know what to do, which was why I now found myself on the front steps of Higgins' home. The door swung open wide and the face of Mr. Higgins with his morning cup of coffee in his hands stood staring back at me.

"I figured it would involve you after I heard the police sirens last night." He brought the cup of coffee to his mouth and took a big gulp. "Come in. I'm sure you are here to ask my wife questions."

I pushed into their home as I nodded in agreement. I was indeed here to seek some advice from Mrs. Higgins.

"Good morning, Mr. Higgins."

"Yes, morning. I miss when everything was quiet in

this town and I could enjoy my days. The wife is in the kitchen still eating breakfast."

He did not need to motion me to the kitchen; I was familiar enough with their home. Instead, he headed to the living room to turn on the television. As I entered the kitchen, Mrs. Higgins sat at the table, writing in her journal.

"Good morning, Kat. How are you this fine morning?"

She turned away from her journal to look at me. A smile was already on her face, and I could see the twinkle in her eyes. I just knew it had to be related to the fact that there was another mystery needing to be solved. Something I was less than thrilled about because I was involved yet again.

I sat down at the table and poured myself a glass of juice. They had been expecting me, because a third glass was already present on the table. It shouldn't have shocked me, but it stirred a little feeling of surprise. But of course, Mrs. Higgins knew I would stop by.

"What can I do for you today?"

"I'm sure you heard all the noise from last night."

She nodded her head while taking a sip of her drink. "I think everyone on the block could hear the police sirens as they went about inspecting Lucy Walker's home."

"Right. It was a home burglary."

"Of course. It makes sense since they are out of town. Let me guess, her jewelry is missing?"

"Yes. Does everyone know she had expensive jewelry at home?"

"Of course everyone knows about the jewelry. Who wouldn't brag about owning those expensive gems?"

I didn't know.

"If everyone knew about them, then anybody could have stolen them."

Mrs. Higgins placed her glass on the table before jotting down something quickly in her journal.

"Right. We have a mystery. Well, actually you have a mystery."

"You won't help?"

"I promised the husband I wouldn't solve any more crimes. But we can spend time together. And if during those times you want to ask questions, who am I to say no?" Nonchalantly, she poked at the food on her plate before taking a bite. Like she just didn't sign herself up to help me solve a burglary.

"So what do I do? The police are looking into it, but if it's not solved before she gets back, I'm not sure how she will react."

"Of course, I would be afraid, too. Lucy likes having her life in order, and having her stuff stolen is the direct opposite of that. But first, have you heard about Delores Fuller?"

I shook my head no. I had heard the name Delores Fuller muttered around town, but I knew little about her. Other than she had money, and she lived in town but kept to herself. I wasn't sure if I had seen her before, so for all I knew she could be made up.

"It seems they also broke into her house. She is also missing expensive pieces of jewelry like our neighbor Lucy."

"Wait, multiple burglaries in the neighborhood?"

"It would appear so."

"Why am I just now hearing about this?"

"Because they like to keep things a bit hush-hush around here. After all, we are supposedly a very peaceful community."

I pondered the information Mrs. Higgins shared as I took another sip of my juice. There had been another burglary in town, and it had happened to Delores Fuller. If I could talk to her, then maybe I could get more information to piece together who had done this. Because from where I stood now, I knew little about the people Lucy Walker interacted with. But I did know that she enjoyed being on a schedule and going to the gym.

"All right then, I guess I will stop by her house and see if she knows anything."

"You can't just walk up to her house, especially after everything that's happened."

"Then what am I to do?"

"Go to the library."

"The library?"

"Why yes, Delores is a huge fan of books. She goes

to the library often to restock on things to read before going back into her cave for the next few days."

"How do you know this information?"

"Just because I don't solve mysteries anymore doesn't mean I stopped noticing things." She smiled. "Off you go. If you delay much longer, you will miss your chance of seeing her for several days." Mrs. Higgins waved goodbye before going back to writing in her journal.

I didn't have time to dawdle if I wanted a chance of solving this mystery before Lucy Walker got home. With a destination in mind, I headed to the front door to leave. I passed by Mr. Higgins, who now rested on the couch. Coffee still in hand, but no doubt no longer hot.

"Have a good day, Kat," he called out, his eyes never leaving the television.

"You too."

"Hope you and my wife aren't up to no good."

I shut the door behind me without saying another word.

Chapter Four

I made a quick pit stop at the café where I'd previously had my date, since my stomach had made itself known that it wasn't happy about the lack of fuel. After I picked up a snack, I made my way to the library. With muffin in hand, I proceed up the stairs and upon entering the front door, walked through a second set of doors and into the common area where people could sit and read if they liked. Not too far back into the building, was the checkout counter, where Mr. Tempest spent most of his time.

He enjoyed manning the desk in order to monitor everyone, while his wife did most of the shelving and organizing in the library. It was a family-run endeavor and with the passing of his daughter several years back, it would go next to his grandchildren to take over and keep the tradition going. That is, if they wanted to.

"Good morning, Mr. Tempest!" I called out as I

closed the door behind me, being sure to give a friendly wave in greeting.

"Is that a muffin in your hand?"

"It is."

"You know the rules. No food or drinks in the library."

"Right, I forgot. It has been a bit since I was last here."

"You need more books in your life. Stop by the library more often."

With a strained smile, I made my way back outside.

I munched on my muffin as I sat down on the steps, doing my best trying to finish it quickly without choking. It was a beautiful day outside. Barely any clouds filled the sky and the sun shone brightly, casting everything in a glow. Too bad I wouldn't have time to enjoy the day more as I had a crime to solve, and I was on a tight deadline because Lucy Walker was only a few days away from returning home. I stuffed the last piece of my muffin in my mouth and dusted my hands on my knees as I headed back into the library.

"All done." I waved both my hands in the air to show that they were muffin-free.

"Good."

Mr. Tempest turned around from the front counter to head into his office and promptly closed the door behind him. Well, I guess I wouldn't be able to ask him where to find Delores Fuller or if she was even here at this very moment. I strolled around the library, trying to see if there was anyone I could ask about where to locate the other victim. Mrs. Higgins seemed sure that I could find her here today, so I would just have to trust her.

"Didn't expect to see you here." A very familiar voice spoke up.

"I don't talk to cats in public." I hissed as I ran my hand along a row of books. It was the reference section of the library. I paused, my fingers hovering over an encyclopedia. That would be the last thing I would want to check out.

"Calm down, there is barely anyone here," Rusty said. He maneuvered himself to sit by my feet and looked straight up at me.

"Liking your new home?"

"It's quite nice."

"Do you know Delores Fuller?" I asked, as I crouched to be closer to Rusty's height.

"Finally taking the case? Lady was complaining about how you never followed up with her."

"Lady?"

I knew lots of ladies, but not someone who actually went by Lady. I had been approached by a cat about a robbery—was that who he was talking about?

"The brown and white cat?"

"Yes, that is Lady. The most beautiful Himalayan cat to walk this Earth."

I tried to stifle my laughter, not wanting to have Mr.

Tempest track me down for being loud in a library. It seemed Rusty had developed a crush.

I reached out and ruffled his fur, as I couldn't help but tease him. "Aw, that's cute. Rusty has a crush."

"It's not just a crush, she is the love of my life."

That was on the extreme side. I wasn't sure how long Rusty had known Lady, but I didn't think it was long. But who was I to question cat love?

"Right ... Is that how Lady knows I can talk to cats? Because you told her?"

"Of course. She came to me with a problem, and I knew the perfect person to help her."

"You can't just offer my services to others. You shouldn't be telling people about me understanding cats at all!"

"I didn't tell people, I told cats. Plus, I didn't offer it for free, she paid for your services."

Again with this mysterious payment. Lady had mentioned she had paid for my services with jewels, but I hadn't received them. And now Rusty was saying the same thing. Not bothering to question the so-called mystery payment as it wouldn't help solve the case, I focused on the real reason I was here.

"Back to Delores Fuller. Where can I find her?"

"Romance section. She spends most of her time over there."

I thanked Rusty and stood back up to make my way over to the romance section. The library wasn't huge; it really only consisted of one floor. Somebody did mention a basement once, but it seemed to be more of a myth than a fact. Mr. Tempest would never confirm or deny the existence of a bottom floor.

"Fiction ... fantasy ... historical ... ah-ha, romance!" After finding the fiction section of the library it was easy to locate the romance section. But as I wove in between the aisles, I saw no other human present except for myself.

"It's you."

This time it wasn't Rusty who spoke out loud, it was his crush and the cat from before, Lady.

"Hi."

"What do you want?"

"You hired me, I'm here to see what the case is about."

"Now you want to work the case?" She twirled on her feet to start walking away, obviously annoyed by my dismissal of her previous attempts to get my attention.

"Yes, I heard you had a burglary, and now expensive jewels are missing."

"Indeed, but I don't need your help."

I followed behind Lady as she walked down the aisles of the library. She had definitely been here before because she knew exactly where to step and how to maneuver her body to allow her to slip out of sight for a second only to reappear again seconds later.

"Honestly, I thought I got scammed out of my payment."

Again with the mention of a payment.

"Right. Your payment. I never received it."

"Not my fault. I paid it, take it up with your boss."

My face scrunched up. Who was she talking about? "My boss?"

"So first you say you didn't get my payment and now you don't know who your boss is? Humans."

"Right, your owner Delores. Where can I find her?"

It seemed that every cat that I met had a bit of snarkiness in them. I still had no idea who she was referring to when she mentioned my boss. But I had bigger things to focus on than her thinking she'd actually hired me to solve this case. I needed to solve this case before Lucy Walker came back and realized her home had been broken into.

"She has probably already left." Lady stopped walking as she had found who she was looking for— Rusty. Not her owner Delores, like I'd thought.

"What do you mean she left?"

"Really? Again. Left, as in not here."

"Where is she going?"

"Home. You might be able to still catch her though."

Without needing any other prompting, I hurried to the front of the library where indeed there was no lady outside. Mr. Tempest was out of his office now, and cleaning up the counter.

"Did Delores Fuller just leave?"

"Yes."

Chapter Five

I ran down the front steps of the library, hoping to catch Delores. I didn't know what she looked like, but hopefully something would just click, and I'd be able to locate her. As I scanned the streets, there was a lady walking away with a stack of books in her hands. Her long black hair swayed from side to side as she maneuvered her head to peer around her stack of books, since it was taller than her head. I ran after her, hoping that she was the person I was looking for.

"Delores Fuller?"

She turned back to look at me around her stack of books, and I shot my hand in the air, waving to get her attention. But instead of stopping, she turned back around and sped up a little. Yet, she could only go so fast with a stack of books in her hands.

"Delores, right?" I asked as I swung out in front of her, blocking her path and causing her to stop walking.

"Yes," she quietly answered, not peeking out from behind the books she carried.

"This is going to sound weird and normally I would not start off with this, but I heard you had some jewelry stolen?"

Her body tensed and her shoulders jerked back a little, causing the books to bounce for a brief moment from the movement.

"No reason to be alarmed," I spoke as my hands came out to brace the books if they dared to fall. "My neighbor's house was broken into as well and I am just trying to put the pieces together."

"Yes, the cops are looking into it."

She sidestepped me and continued down the street, but I didn't give up. I joined her at her side, as I didn't want to lose my opportunity to gain more information. She was the only other person impacted by the burglary and so the only other person I could ask. If she couldn't help me get my questions answered, then no one else could. Except maybe the talking cats, but they were also the reason I kept getting in these kinds of messes. If Rusty had never appeared at my doorstep that fateful day Rose Hastings was murdered, then maybe all of this could have been avoided. I focused on the lady next to me again as I shook the thoughts of talking cats from my mind.

"Here, let me help you. It's the least I could do since I'm trying to ask a bunch of questions."

She pushed her stack of books at me, and I

grabbed the top half of it. Now she was only carrying half the books, and would be able to see in front of her. We continued down the path, but she didn't volunteer any information regarding the break-in. I guessed I would have to start with my questioning, as I had a case to solve.

"Can you tell me when the break-in happened?

No response.

"Did you see the person who did it?" I paused before continuing. "I didn't. By the time I noticed the burglary, the jewelry thief was already long gone."

I had hoped by providing some of my information, she would offer a bit of hers. But again it was not the case, and she continued on walking down the street in silence. At this rate, our walk would be nothing more than a one-sided conversation. Which was the direct opposite of what I wanted and needed.

"I met Lady in the library today, Rusty seems smitten with her."

"He is. It's quite cute," she replied, bringing a smile to my face.

I had finally cracked the code! It just had to include the talking cats. It seemed I could never distance myself from them. "Rusty showed up at my doorstep after his owner died. I gave him to Mr. Tempest. I figured his grandchildren would like the company."

"That was smart and very nice of you to do. Rusty is great company to have while I'm in the library."

"It's pretty crazy, really. Out of all the houses on the

block he could've gone to, he shows up at mine! It was also shocking when Rose Hastings died, but it seems trouble has been finding me more lately."

She slammed to a halt and whirled to look at me, causing me to stop walking.

"That wasn't you who killed her, right?"

I was at a loss for words as I looked at Delores. It was true what Mrs. Higgins had said, that she didn't get out much.

"No, the culprit is already in jail."

As I mulled over her words more, I let loose a laugh. It was ridiculous to think that I killed someone! I wasn't crazy! Except for being able to talk to cats, but that was a different kind of crazy.

"I just helped solve the case. It turns out it was motivated by money."

"Sorry. Mr. Tempest had mentioned she had died, and your name came up in the conversation. I just wasn't paying attention to the entire story."

Delores continued her stroll forward, and I followed suit. "So now you are solving the burglary?"

"I don't have a choice. I was housesitting for Lucy Walker, and I'm afraid she is going to go crazy when she finds out. I would rather have some good news for her. Fewer things for her to be mad about."

"You sound like you could be a character in some of the books I read."

"Oh, that sounds cool. But I doubt my life is as interesting as theirs."

"You solve mysteries. Now all you need is romance!"

I snorted at her words. My attempt at romance had been ruined when her very own cat had banged against the window at the café. Maybe I would've had a romance if it wasn't for her feline.

"I don't think there will be romance in my future."

"Well, if you can't have romance, you can be in the mystery books I read. You just need a talking animal."

My stomach dropped and my palms started to sweat, making it harder to carry the books. Those weren't the words I wanted to hear. I didn't want anyone to know about my situation with understanding cats. That would only lead to bad news.

"Talking dogs are my favorite."

"Dogs?"

"Dogs that help solve crimes."

I was more of a dog person and having the ability to talk to dogs seemed far better deal than talking to cats.

"We're here."

I took in my surroundings as it seemed we had arrived at her house. I had never ventured to her home before, since I had not met her before. Her home was definitely on the bigger side and if she picked up her home, moved it to my block, it would stick out like a sore thumb. I was surprised I had never noticed this home before. It could have been because the looming trees in front covered a portion of the home from sight.

"Okay, do you want me to bring your books in?"

I had already intruded too much and didn't dare ask to be invited in so I could ask more questions.

"No. Give me one moment."

I set my stack of books back onto hers and she fished the key out of her pocket and pushed open the door while doing an incredible balancing trick that could only come from repeated practice. She unlocked the door and proceeded inside.

Just as I turned to head back home, Delores poked her head back outside.

"Actually, would you like a cup of tea?"

I looked around as I sat in the living room of Delores' house. It contained furniture that I wasn't sure I could find easily if I was to search the typical stores. Maybe if I ventured through several thrift stores and scavenged garage sales I might, but that was a big maybe, as some of her things looked ancient.

With a cup of tea still in hand, I grabbed a cookie off the tray on the coffee table. It was a pleasant home and hopefully I would I have a chance to see the whole house. Maybe Delores and I could become friends, as we looked close in age. Feet padded against the wooden floor as she came back into the living room. She had left to fill up the teapot to ensure we could have a few more cups of tea.

"The cookies are fantastic, what are they?"

"The ones you get on the airplanes. I don't travel often so it reminds me of going on an adventure."

Delores filled up her cup of tea before maneuvering to sit in the chair opposite of the coffee table. In a neon-yellow chair that clashed with the darker tones in the room.

"I have a few additional questions about the burglary."

"I will do my best to help."

I scooted to sit at the edge of the couch and prepared to question Delores once more. It was finally time to figure out the details of this case. I imagined pulling out a notepad and pen like I was a police detective, about to uncover the biggest scoop of the century.

"Did you see who did it?"

"No, I wasn't home."

"Were you at the library when it happened?"

"Yes, every time."

"Every time?" I questioned.

"Yes, someone has broken into my dwelling at least twice."

Now that was something different. I was sure Lucy Walker's residence was only broken into once unless I had been completely oblivious. The night before the break-in, nothing had been broken in Lucy's home. Perhaps the person had only hit Lucy's residence once because there wasn't a lot of valuables. While Delores must have a decent number of valuables for someone to come back a second time. There were a lot of vintage items in the house that could sell for a decent price if someone tried to resell them.

"Was jewelry the only thing taken?"

"I would say no. They took anything with gems in it, though."

"Can you give me an example?"

"Lady's water and feeding bowls had some gems on them, and now they're gone. I didn't notice the missing items till she threw a fit."

My eyes rolled on instinct. Of course, it was the cat who had noticed. That just proved my previous thoughts that if I didn't have the ability to talk to cats, I wouldn't be in half the situations I seemed to get myself into lately.

"After you called the cops, did they say anything?"

"No, they must review the catalog of items that have documented to be in the house. I guess there are a lot of expensive things that I inherited from my family."

She leaned forward to take a cookie from the tray and began munching away. I reclined back and took a moment to process her words.

They had already hit her residence twice, but no doubt there were still priceless items throughout the home left to be picked. But now that the cops were involved, there would be no way whoever it was would hit the same place again, especially so soon after. Unless the criminal wasn't the sharpest crayon in the box. The jewel thief would need a new target to go after and I wasn't sure who that might be.

"Was that all of your questions?"

"Perhaps did you invite someone over who might have acted a bit suspicious or weird?"

She looked over the top of her cup of tea as she took a sip.

"Other than you, no."

My face heated a little at her remark. I guess one could call me weird since I had practically run after her to get information. Then I had mentioned that my neighbor had been murdered and another neighbor had her home broken into. Those things didn't happen randomly—I was probably cursed or had some very bad karma. Good thing she didn't know about the cats, or I would most definitely be labeled as suspicious.

"Well, I think that is all of my questions. I really appreciate this, and it was nice meeting you, Delores Fuller." I set my cup of tea on the coffee table, stood up, and stretched my hand out for a handshake.

I wasn't able to solve the case yet, but I was a step closer. After shaking her hand goodbye, I turned and headed toward the front door. I needed to figure out what to do next and that would require the mind of a detective. Or at least someone who was married to one. But it could wait till tomorrow.

Chapter Six

The television was on low in the background as I sat on the couch, staring at the screen of my phone as my best friend talked away. She was going on about some new restaurants she had found in her area, but I was only half listening. My mind was still trying to connect the dots in order to solve the theft case. Upon my return home from Delores Fuller's home, I had found Lola waiting for me in front of the door. She was a bit annoyed when I'd arrived. She was doing her best to uphold her end of the arrangement we had in place, and I was nowhere to be found. While I wanted her to come home every few days it didn't mean that I must be home at all times. I could not predict when she decided to show up, and I still had a life to attend to.

"You seem like you have a lot on your mind."

"Not really." That was a huge lie.

"Are you sure?" she countered.

"There was another incident that happened a few days ago."

"And let me guess. It somehow involves you?"

"In a way. Someone broke into Lucy Walker's home. She's the lady I'm housesitting for while she is on vacation."

"What did they take? Is the house trashed?"

"The house is fine, but all the jewelry has been taken."

"I'm not sure what's worse, a trashed house or missing jewelry that probably cost a ton!"

I let out a sigh at her words and sank into the couch. Both scenarios were bad and if I had the choice, I would avoid either of them.

"So what are you going to do about it?"

"Why do you think I have to do something about it?"

"Because it happened on your watch! And Lucy Walker doesn't seem like the forgiving type."

"She's right, you know."

My eyes drifted to the ones staring at me from the floor. Lola had been listening in on the conversation I was having with her mother. But I did not respond to her—I still hadn't told my friend that I could talk to cats. After the incident at the café, when I had talked to Lady in front of other people, it was now my mission to avoid talking to cats any time others might see. Eventually, someone would call me a cat lady, at the rate I was attracting cats. That was a nickname I never thought I would gain. Just thinking about it sent a shiver down my spine.

"Hey, I've actually got to go. Talk in a few days like normal?"

"Of course."

After hanging up the phone and putting it down, I could now talk to the cats without others overhearing.

"I don't understand cats."

"We aren't that complex."

My brows crinkled in confusion at Lola's words, who in return just lifted her front paw and started licking it.

"Cats aren't complex? You can talk! You have me solving crimes, including a murder. And let's not forget other cats can apparently hire me."

"Weird."

Now totally uninterested in our conversation, Lola excused herself from the living room to do who-knew-what somewhere else in the house. I seriously didn't understand cats. But right now, I didn't have time to think any more about it. I needed to focus and go over the information I had learned so far. I still had a case to solve.

Just thinking about everything relating to my new investigation exhausted me. Maybe it was my body's way of telling me I wasn't cut out for this kind of life. So I made myself a promise this would be the last case I would work. I needed to get back to my peaceful life.

And besides, the odds that another crime would happen in this town were very low. Or at least that was what I told myself. I let out a nervous laugh and headed to my bedroom to cash in on some rest. No point in dwelling on those thoughts when I could instead just relax and go to sleep—it was night time after all. My eyes became heavy as soon as I slid in between the sheets. It didn't take long to drift off from the real world and enter dreamland.

I was pulled from my sleep as a loud crash echoed throughout my home. Whatever the cats were up to, it could wait till morning. I wasn't in the mood to deal with it right now. But the noises continued and were followed by loud meows and hisses. I groaned and rolled over, picked up my pillow, and slammed it over my face to help muffle the noise.

"What are you doing?" Luna said.

I shifted the pillow, my eyes opening to see her green eyes staring at me.

"What? I'm sleeping." I hissed. All I wanted a peaceful night of rest, but the cats seemed to have other plans.

"Why?"

"Why what?"

"Do you normally sleep while people break into your home?"

My body jerked up to a sitting position, the pillow falling to the side to land squarely on Luna. She wiggled out, but I was already throwing the sheets off as I scrambled out of bed, only to cover her once more under the blankets as I landed in a heap on the floor.

"Stop that!" she yelled, her body slithering under the sheets as she tried to find her way out.

"Sorry!" I croaked. I ran from the bedroom to the living room, where the noise was coming from.

As I slid into the room, my body froze at the scene in front of me. Zaira darted around like a ninja, swiping at the person's ankles. They attempted to kick her, but she was too fast and would come right back with another swipe. Lola, on the other hand, was a demon, clinging to the person's back as he wildly tried to swat at her. She didn't like having her nails trimmed, and I knew from firsthand experience that they were sharp. Her claws allowed her to cling to his back as she nipped at him when she could.

"What …" I mumbled, in complete shock.

But I soon regretted my decision as the person turned to face me. I instinctively looked down at my hands, which held no weapon. And I definitely didn't have any claws like Lola and Zaira, so I was pretty much defenseless.

I did the only thing I knew how to do. I slid my foot back and crouched, arms wildly flailing in front of my body. They did this in the movies. I wasn't too sure how effective it would be, but it was better than nothing.

"Ouch!"

The person before me screamed as they finally were able to grasp Lola and throw her off. She rebounded to land on her feet and stood in front of me. Her fur stuck out in all directions, like she was still on high alert. Zaira also paused in her attacks as Lola, who provided the main distractions, was thrown off. She slid off into a corner of the room, waiting for the next opportunity to join the fray once more. But that opportunity wouldn't come—the person ran for the front door and then right out of the house. Even though he'd vanished, I stayed in my position, not moving for a few moments, just in case.

"You look ridiculous," Lola spoke as her fur started to settle back down.

"What happened?"

"Pretty sure you just saw what happened."

"But why?"

"It was a human, so wouldn't you know more than I?"

Finally moving out of the awkward ninja stance I had taken, I slumped to the ground. My chest heaved as my mind caught up to everything that had just happened. Someone had broken into my home, for who knew what reasons. And I had walked out to confront the person with no way to protect myself! Tears pooled in my eyes and started to spill. I didn't have the energy to contain them.

"What is wrong with you?"

"I could have died!"

"Aren't you glad I came back today and not another

day?" Lola asked as she waddled off to do her own thing once more.

I was a mess on the floor, in the middle of my living room. Luna was still probably in my bed, not caring about everything that had just unfolded. What had I done to deserve all this bad karma in my life?

Chapter Seven

S un pierced through the window of my bedroom as I lay under the covers, pillow tightly clutched to my chest as I stared at the ceiling. It was the same position I had taken after everything happened last night; I hadn't moved once. My body was too tense to let sleep take over, so falling asleep had been impossible. The best I could do to help ease my mind was to stare at the ceiling all night.

"Are you dead?"

"Leave me alone."

"You act like it's the end of the world."

"Well, what am I supposed to do?"

"Report it to the police."

I dragged the pillow from my chest to my face, took a deep breath, and let out a very frustrated scream.

"That won't solve anything."

I threw the pillow off to the side since it didn't seem

I was going to be allowed to wallow in self-pity. Lola dodged the pillow, unlike Luna the night before. With a slew of curses released under my breath, I rolled out of bed. Nothing made sense. It was one bad thing after another and now someone had broken into my home. I just couldn't catch a break.

Taking the cat's advice, I would go to the police station to report the crime. I needed to get out of the house anyway. After a quick stop in the bathroom to freshen up to avoid looking like a zombie, I was ready to head outside.

"Where are you going?" Luna asked.

"To the police station." With that, I closed the door behind me.

I did my best to not think about the events of last night or the case I needed to solve as I walked to the police station. I just wanted to enjoy a peaceful walk before things got all crazy again. Lost in thought, I arrived at the front steps of the police station, one of the older buildings in the city. It had two stories with windows lining the front of the building, allowing for a perfect view of the street. The oddest thing about the police station was that since it was old, the building was very narrow.

Joe Grey was working the front desk. He stayed seated in his chair but offered a wave as I entered the building. He preferred to say sitting unless he was fighting crime because of his advanced age. He was the friendly neighborhood grandpa with his matching gray hair and mustache. I doubted he was solving much crime nowadays, though. He had to be at least in his late sixties, yet somehow still on the force.

"Afternoon! What can I do for you today, Kat?" His voice carried over the tall desk even though I could only see his eyes and the top of his head from my position near the front door. Joe Grey was not a tall man.

I made my way over and leaned on the desk as I tapped on it, my nerves showing. "Got a crime to report."

"A crime, you say? What happened?"

"Someone broke into my home."

"That sure is a crime, all right. Make your way over to Detective Davidson and he will be able to help you out."

I waved goodbye to Joe and started to head up to the second floor where everyone had their offices, but then I paused

"Detective Davidson?" I inquired. It was a name I wasn't familiar with.

"New on the force. Can't miss him, probably the only one in his twenties here." Joe chuckled, waving me on to continue up the stairs, which I did.

It seemed the city had hired a new police officer. I wondered if it was before or after everything that had happened recently?

Upon reaching the second floor, I scanned the open office area. I hoped he would be visible, and I wouldn't have to search the offices in the back. I walked down the hallway and peered at the few desks that had people seated at them.

"Kat Jones?" a voice called out from the far back corner.

I searched out where the voice had come from—a desk with a huge plant on the corner and an equally huge computer monitor which blocked whoever was sitting there. But then a man stood and waved his hand at me, and now I could see him clearly. So this was the new guy, Detective Davidson.

"Please, sit." He motioned to the chair in front of his desk before taking his own seat. I waited to see what questions he would have for me as I slid into the offered chair.

"Joe called to let me know you were on your way up."

I nodded my head. Couldn't have just anyone walking around the police station, even if it was a small town where most of the people knew each other.

"A break-in, huh? Can you tell me what happened? Were you home? Did they take anything?" He rattled off a few more questions, but it was hard to follow him, as he didn't pause to let me answer the ones he'd already asked.

Detective Davidson fiddled around in his desk drawer, as if trying to find something. As he continued to ramble, he pulled out each drawers of his desk, continuing his search. Finally he pulled out a journal, grabbed a pen from a container on his desk, and smiled at me, waiting for my answers. In return, all I offered was a raised eyebrow. I wasn't sure how new he was, but I hoped this wasn't his first case. He reached his hand behind his neck to scratch in embarrassment.

"This is only my second case."

Well, it was better than it being his first case. The million questions he had shot off in rapid-fire succession had kind of given him away. But at least he was enthusiastic about his job.

"So tell me about the break-in." He asked once more, this time not following up with any additional questions, which allowed me time to provide some information.

"It was late at night. Not sure when exactly, as I was asleep, but it was probably close to midnight or the early hours of the morning?"

He nodded his head and scribbled away in his notebook. Then he paused and looked at me thoughtfully.

"You were home when it happened?"

"Yes."

"Oh, that's not good," he whispered under his breath but I could still hear him. "Tell me more," he continued.

"I'm pretty sure the cats roughed the person up pretty good."

"Cats? Do your cats normally attack people?"

I paused to think about his question. Did cats

normally attack people like that, or was it because they were special and I could understand them? Who really knows, I wasn't an expert on cats. I just shrugged my shoulders. Cats were weird animals, after all. Who knew what was normal behavior for them.

"Did the person steal anything?"

"I don't think so. The cats got to them before they had a chance, I believe."

He nodded his head again and started writing again in his journal before once more pausing to look at me.

"Um, do you think it's okay for me to investigate the house? The cats won't attack me, right?" he asked a bit hesitantly. He seemed to be unsure if the cats in the house were vicious, and I couldn't really blame him for wondering. They sure sounded vicious when they fought off an attacker.

"Yes, you are fine to stop by."

His body relaxed at my words. I wasn't sure if he didn't like cats or just didn't want to be on the receiving end of their claws digging into his skin.

"Well, the good news is I doubt you will have another break-in. I'm sure those cats scared off whoever it was enough that they won't want to try again."

He reached for his bag that leaned against his chair and put it on the desktop. He neatly tucked away his journal and the other papers that were on his desk into his bag, and slung it over his shoulder before standing.

"Would you like a ride back home? It would be best to inspect your place while things are still fresh."

I agreed and we headed back down the stairs to make our way outside.

"By chance, are you the same Kat Jones who reported the burglary at a Mrs. Lucy Walker's home?"

"Unfortunately."

"I haven't been able to get in touch with her regarding the theft. She knows her home was broken into, right?"

"I think the place where she is vacationing might have poor cell reception."

I didn't answer the other question. Was it considered lying if I just omitted information? Lying to a police officer was definitely not something someone should do. But telling Lucy Walker all her precious jewelry was in the wind was also something someone should not do. And picking the lesser of the two evils was the best option in this case.

"You know, everyone told me nothing ever happens in this city. But there seems to be a small uptick in crime lately. I wonder what has changed."

Talking cats. That was what had changed. But I couldn't tell him that.

We waved goodbye to Joe Grey who still sat behind his desk as we made our way outside. Detective Davidson let me to one of the unmarked police cars and we headed back to my house.

Chapter Eight

I found myself once more at the Higgins' home staring into the face of Mr. Higgins, who stood on the other side of the doorframe.

"Well, Kat Jones, I heard trouble has found you once more," he said, sipping from his cup. His eyes never left mine as he looked slightly more annoyed more than he usually did. "And now you are on my doorstep once more. What can I help you with?"

"Honey, what are you doing? Let her in!" Mrs. Higgins' voice rang from inside, causing Mr. Higgins to scowl before stepping aside.

With entry now permitted, I walked into their home. He closed the door behind me and made his way back to the living room.

"There used to be only one troublemaker on the block, and now there are two," he muttered under his breath, sitting down on the couch. He no longer paid attention to me, which was my cue to make my way to Mrs. Higgins. She liked to spend most of her time in the breakfast nook in the kitchen. When I walked in, I saw that I'd guessed right; she sat at the table reading a book. When she noticed I'd entered, she closed her book and smiled at me warmly.

"Seems something else has happened. Care to fill me in?" she asked as she pointed to an empty dining room seat as an offer for me to sit down and join her.

I couldn't help but notice the spread of plates and dishes of food on the table. It was a lot for just two people.

"Did I interrupt something?"

"Absolutely not. You are always welcome!"

Was the spread put out because she had been expecting me? I cast a quick glance in her direction; her smile made me really curious. She had a very keen sixth sense and always seemed to know when I was coming over. Or they always set at the table for an extra, in case anybody stopped by. But that was a different type of friendly I wasn't sure existed. No, Mrs. Higgins definitely knew I would come over today.

"Help yourself. We couldn't possibly eat all of this ourselves."

I reached to cut a piece of the cheesecake and place it on the small plate in front of me. It was covered in a thick, purple liquid, which I knew was Mr. Higgins' secret sauce. It definitely felt like Mrs. Higgins had been expecting me today.

"So what happened? There was a bit of noise last night then the police dropped you off today."

"Someone broke into my home."

"Oh no, are you okay?"

"Yes. Shaken, but all right. The cats definitely did a number on the intruder though."

"Having pets is truly a blessing."

Having pets could be a blessing if they didn't talk. Those types of pets were a different story, and I still wasn't sure how I felt about it other than I was pretty sure I wasn't a cat person. But I had to hand it to them, because they saved me last time. I also had an inkling that if I didn't have these cats, then I wouldn't be in so much trouble.

"Do you think it's the same person who broke into Lucy Walker's home?" she continued.

"I think so. But why break into my home? I have nothing of value."

"Maybe they got word that you were looking into things. You drew too much attention and turned yourself into a target."

I would have to agree with what she said. I didn't much have time to think about why the person had broken into my home—I was still too busy coming to terms with the fact that someone had actually done it in the first place.

Mrs. Higgins took a bite of her own piece of cheesecake before picking up her wineglass. She swirled the wine in the glass a bit before taking a long sip, then placed the glass back down on the table.

"If the person is going to come after you, don't you think you should go after them?"

"I was just looking for information, I don't actually want to be the person to capture him."

"Even after the death of Rose Hastings, you don't appreciate the thrill of a great mystery?"

I raised my eyebrow at Mrs. Higgins as I continued to eat my cheesecake. She seemed to understand my response, which was that solving mysteries was not my cup of tea. And if everyone could kindly let me have my peace, along with the talking cats, that would be wonderful.

"Well then, I guess I have no other choice than to help you out."

"Why does it feel like you wanted to help, and are only pretending to be forced to help?"

Mrs. Higgins leaned back in her seat and picked up her glass of wine.

"Volunteer to solve a mystery? Heavens no, my husband would have my head. I'm just helping out a neighbor."

She brought the glass of wine once more to her lips and took a small sip.

"I can't have too much if we want to plan a capture." Mrs. Higgins spoke.

"And how do we plan to capture this person?"

"It's simple, really."

Mrs. Higgins leaned forward to set her glass of wine on the table before getting up of her seat. She left the kitchen without answering my question. Was I supposed to follow or wait here? I didn't have to wonder long, because after a few seconds her head popped back around the corner.

"Honestly, if we are going to capture a criminal, you are going to need to keep up."

I guessed I was supposed to follow, after all. I shoved a few more bites of cheesecake into my mouth and followed her.

"Honey, what are you up to?" Mr. Higgins eyed us suspiciously as we walked past him and down the hall.

"Nothing!" Mrs. Higgins called out as she grabbed my arm and pulled me the remaining distance to their bedroom before shutting the door quickly behind us. She went to her closet and she riffled around, looking for something. I wasn't sure what she was looking for, but apparently it was an item that would help us capture a criminal. Maybe it was a baseball bat or something. I may not have claws but having a bat would work. Instead, she returned with a small box in her hands.

"This is going to help us solve this mystery."

My eyes bulged as she slowly opened the box. It was a jewelry set—a very expensive one at that, judging by the way it shone.

"Diamonds, to draw out our little thief."

My hands reached out of their own free will,

enchanted by the shiny gems in front of me. No wonder there was a jewel thief in town. Shiny jewelry had the ability to cast a haze of desire over someone's eyes. All I wanted to do was touch the breathtaking jewels in her hands.

"What exactly are we doing with the diamonds?"

"We are going to go out on the town, of course. We don't know who our thief is, so we need to draw him out."

"So let him see this set on you and make you the next target? Sounds kind of crazy."

"But it will work."

Mrs. Higgins grabbed the box of jewelry from my hands before shoving it back into her closet. Then she headed to the bedroom door, opened it, and motioned for me to follow her. As we walked down the hallway to the front door, Mr. Higgins sent us suspicious looks every step of the way.

"Stop by tomorrow morning."

"Why is she coming back tomorrow morning?" Mr. Higgins asked from his position on the couch. Paying no mind to him, Mrs. Higgins leaned in, brushing her hair behind her ear before whispering.

"We've got a thief to catch."

"What are you up to?" he asked.

I shot a smile at Mr. Higgins and waved goodbye to Mrs. Higgins before heading outside to go back to my home. I could see why Mr. Higgins suspected his wife was up to something. Trouble landed on my front steps despite me not wanting anything to do with it. Mrs. Higgins, on the other hand? She seemed to run straight into trouble despite Mr. Higgins' protests. I couldn't help but wonder what she had been like when she was younger.

Chapter Nine

The sun was shining its wonderful rays on my face as I made the short walk over to the Higgins' home. I wasn't sure what we were going to do today, only that we were going to go looking for a thief. How? I didn't know. I only knew that Mrs. Higgins requested I meet her at her home in the morning.

First Lucy Walker's home was broken into while she was out of town and while I was house sitting. I was motivated to find who the thief was because being on the receiving end of Lucy's temper when she found out her precious jewelry had been stolen was not my idea of fun. Then I found out about Delores Fuller— that her home had been broken into before Lucy Walker's home was. Not only broken into once, but at least twice! There probably would have been a third break-in if Delores didn't call the police for the thief would have thought they were getting away with their crime. She may have also avoided it because I had drawn the attention of our burglar, despite not having a single piece of expensive jewelry in my home. I definitely didn't make jewelry a common part of my wardrobe.

I knocked on the Higgins' front door after covering the short distance between our homes. Being next door neighbors came in handy when I needed to seek out advice. The door opened, and I stared at Mrs. Higgins. Her hair, which usually worn down, was pulled back, allowing the earrings she wore to be on full display. The sun shone on the diamond earrings and they gleamed so brightly that I had to avert my gaze.

Instead of wearing simple clothes like a blouse and pants, today she wore a dress, as if she was going to a cocktail party. But I was one hundred percent sure we weren't going to a cocktail party. I looked down at my own clothes and compared myself to her. I thought we were going to go capture a thief, but obviously, I hadn't understood what exactly we were doing. My jeans were a little short and showed my ankles. My shirt was slightly tucked in, but it was a simple white T-shirt. As I stood next to Mrs. Higgins, I wasn't sure how to compare our outfits, but it definitely didn't look like we were going to the same place.

I looked at her. She wore a pair of strapless low elegant heels. Her dress was a simple, white one that showed off her collarbones and went to her knees.

Because of that, the diamond necklace was on full display and seemed to shine even brighter than before against the white of the dress. And to finally pull it all together, over the dress she wore a blazer that looked to be bedazzled with white jewels on every space possible. with jewels all over it. So if the thief didn't notice the diamonds right away, the shininess of the blazer would certainly draw their eyes in. Then they would be forced to notice the diamonds.

"How do I look?" she asked as she did a small twirl to show off her outfit.

"I thought we were going to capture the—"

Mrs. Higgins' reached out her hand and covered my mouth to prevent me from saying the word thief. Just in time, too, because Mr. Higgins' head popped out from behind the door frame just then.

"I thought you were going to a party. Kat is definitely not dressed for a party," he said as he eyed me up and down and took in my outfit.

"That's just how her generation dresses."

I let loose a laugh as he shot his wife a crazy look.

"Are you about to stick your nose into something it shouldn't be in?"

"Honestly honey, you should have more faith in me."

Mrs. Higgins walked outside to join me on the porch. She hooked her arm into mine and walked us away, leaving Mr. Higgins standing in the doorway by himself.

"I want no part in this trouble you are surely brewing!" he called out.

Mrs. Higgins only waved goodbye, not even stopping to turn around.

"What exactly are we doing? Should I change?"

"Absolutely not. All eyes need to be on me, after all."

That was fine with me.

"First stop is the café. We can't solve a mystery on an empty stomach."

We opted to walk instead of driving over to the café. It wasn't super far, and Mrs. Higgins wanted to make sure she was seen out and about wearing her precious diamonds.

"Did you sleep okay after everything that has happened?"

"It was different, but knowing the cats were there helped tremendously."

"That's very good to hear." She patted my arm in comfort.

Sleeping in my home after a break-in had been odd but knowing I wasn't alone and that the cats lurked in the dark, ready to attack anyone who entered, allowed sleep to come more easily.

Mrs. Higgins dropped my arm as she pushed open the door to the café. She seemed to grab the attention of everyone who was in the place, if the number of dropped jaws was any indication. Even though she was the center of attention, she strolled right up to the counter as if she didn't have a care in the world. I stayed a few paces behind.

"Good morning, Daniel!"

The guy behind the counter gave Mrs. Higgins a smile. "You are looking absolutely amazing today, Mrs. Higgins! Not that you don't always look amazing." His light blue eyes twinkled at her.

She laughed and reached across the counter to playfully hit his arm before turning to face me.

"Kat, what would you like?"

"An iced coffee with a breakfast sandwich, please."

She looked up at the wall and stared at the chalkboard menu for only a moment before speaking.

"A hot tea with a breakfast sandwich for me, please."

Daniel quickly got to work making our order, then slid it across the counter after accepting our payment.

"Enjoy, ladies! Again Mrs. Higgins, you are looking beautiful!"

"Stop it!"

Ignoring the playful banter going on in front of me, I grabbed the tray and headed to a table. I sat down and rearranged the items on the tray to ensure Mrs. Higgins' order was in front of her and mine was in front of me.

"You should go on a date with Daniel sometime. He is a very sweet boy."

"I'm not sure. The last date I went on got interrupted, but I think we will go on another soon."

"I didn't know that. Well, if it doesn't work out, give Daniel a call. He is single."

I didn't want to ask how she knew he was single. Even if something were to happen between Daniel and me, it would all come crumbling down once he realized I could talk to cats. I took a sip from my iced coffee as I waited for Mrs. Higgins to have a seat.

"All right, so first, who do we have for suspects?"

"Nobody, honestly."

"Really, Kat? No one gives you the tingles when you think about them being the thief?"

I sat there for a moment, bringing the sandwich to my mouth to have a few bites. As I chewed away, I thought about the people I had crossed so far in the day Of those people, no one gave me the tingles if I considered them to be a secret thief going around breaking into people's homes to steal jewelry. I also didn't think I had a detective's senses, like the lady in front of me.

"Can't say anyone sets off my thief radar."

"It's okay. Once you solve more mysteries your radar for the suspicious will get stronger."

The next bite of my sandwich lodged in my throat briefly at her words. There were going to be no other mysteries for this girl. All I wanted was a peaceful day and not having to worry about the craziness in the world.

"I haven't been able to gather much information so

far. Mr. Higgins has been trying to keep me far away from this. But we should go to the library next."

"Why the library?"

"Because Delores Fuller visits that place frequently, and she was the first victim."

I nodded as I took a sip of my iced coffee. It made sense. Good thing Mrs. Higgins had volunteered to assist with this mystery, because she was already being so useful.

"Let's finish up our food and head on over to the library to visit Mr. Tempest."

Chapter Ten

In order to track a thief, you must figure out how they are picking their targets. Or so Mrs. Higgins stated several times on the way to the library. In order to capture a thief, you must present the thief an opportunity they can't pass up, but it needs to be in a controlled environment. Either Mrs. Higgins walking around in broad daylight with diamonds on full display was a controlled environment, or the controlled environment was coming next. I wasn't sure.

"Are you paying attention? You need to be absorbing this information for your next mystery!" Mrs. Higgins exclaimed with her arm wrapped around mine.

I scrunched my nose up at her comment. Why was everyone thrilled to be solving mysteries? After dropping my arm from Mrs. Higgins, I made my way up the steps of the library first, and opened the door wide for her to enter before following her in. It wasn't Mr. Tempest who stood behind the front desk today, it was his wife.

"Welcome to the library!" Her voice was filled with excitement as she greeted us with a vigorous wave of her arm.

"Why, it has been ages since I last saw you!" said Mrs. Higgins.

"Same to you! You don't come to the library as often as you used to."

"Well, when given the chance to live out your fantasy in real life, wouldn't you pursue that?" Mrs. Higgins laughed.

I stared at the two ladies like I was missing something. Unless Mrs. Higgins meant being married to Mr. Higgins was her fantasy, then absolutely everything she had said made no sense. I was pretty sure Mrs. Higgins' primary source of excitement was knowing almost everything about everyone.

"Is your grumpy husband in?"

"Oh, be nice to him! He should be back up front in a few minutes. I just needed a breather from the cave."

Cave?

It was official—whatever they were talking about made no sense to me; they seemed to be speaking in metaphors. There was no cave under the library.

"All right then, I'm going to have a seat, this is a lot on my poor feet."

"It doesn't help that you are wearing heels. I also

noticed the diamonds—they are beautiful! Is there a special event going on that I didn't know about?"

Taking the compliment in full stride, Mrs. Higgins put her hands behind her ears and flicked the earrings back and forth, allowing the light to bounce off the jewels. She followed with a little twirl, despite the rest of her outfit not having diamonds on it.

"I look pretty nice today, don't I?"

A laugh bubbled up from inside, and I let it burst out. Mrs. Higgins was such a character that being in her presence was never boring. Without waiting for a response, Mrs. Higgins plopped back on the couch in the waiting area. She released a sigh of relief since she was finally off her feet.

"Kat, why don't you look around while I talk to my dear friend?"

She winked few times at me to indicate something, but I wasn't sure what she meant. Was she wanting me to find information in the library on my own? She kept sending subtle winks and nods in my directions as she talked to Mrs. Tempest. She must have had a plan, so it would be best I followed suit. I turned on my heels and headed deeper into the library. The woody smell filled the air, followed by a faint hint of a cat. Where was Rusty? I walked down the aisles and tried to locate the tabby cat and anything that might provide some clues as to who had targeted Delores. When I had come here earlier to talk to Delores, I wasn't looking for clues in the library, just a person.

"Solved the case already?" a familiar voice piped up from behind an aisle.

"No, I haven't."

"You should probably solve the case before they steal something of mine next."

"Do you even have anything worth stealing?"

"That is for you to never find out."

I crouched to be a bit more eye-level with Rusty and gave him some scratches under his chin.

"I hope there won't be another theft anytime soon. I'm currently looking for clues. You wouldn't happen by chance to have any information to share, would you?"

"I sent Lady and her owner to you. Not sure what else I can assist with."

"Turns out Delores Fuller was the first break-in, and Lucy Walker was the second. And then finally, I was the third."

Rusty paused from his attempt to gather more pets to look up at me.

"You are on the target list?"

"Seems so."

"But you don't have any fancy stuff in your house."

"Thanks, Rusty." I rolled my eyes at his comment and tucked my hands back into my lap, no longer offering any types of pets, thanks to the jab he'd just provided.

"Well, Delores Fuller is a regular here. But this Lucy Walker is not."

"The thief did not meet them here."

"It would be safe to assume so."

For that information, I could forgive the jab and placed a kiss on his head. I sprang to my feet and headed back to the front room to meet up with Mrs. Higgins. Maybe she had gathered some information from the Tempest family. But I doubted there would be much information to gather if only one victim came here regularly, and not both. It didn't take long to return to the front of the building and see both Mr. and Mrs. Tempest sitting with Mrs. Higgins. The three of them conversed quietly, and I couldn't hear them as I made my way up to the front.

"Find anything useful, Kat?" Mrs. Higgins called out.

"Only that Lucy doesn't come to the library."

"I could have told you that," Mr. Tempest said. He set his arm on the top of the couch and turned to face me as he spoke.

"Lucy and books are two things that have never gone together. But Lucy goes to the chiropractic office just a few shops away. She always passes by the library on her way."

"Great information as always, my friend."

Mr. Tempest turned his attention from me to Mrs. Higgins and offered her a smile.

"I've learned a thing or two from the best in town."

"Hopefully we will have another best in town soon. What do you say to that, Kat?"

My body tensed up at her words. I wasn't cut out to solve mysteries, and it wasn't something I seemed to be any good at. So all I could offer was a smile to try to hide some of the awkwardness I was feeling.

"Off to the chiropractic office then. Have a wonderful day my friends, I will be sure to visit again soon."

Chapter Eleven

Again, we found ourselves walking down the street to our next destination, courtesy of Mr. Tempest. The city wasn't very big and while driving was quickest way to get around, things weren't bad if walking was the only available mode of transportation.

"So, we are just going to enter every single business we come across to look for clues?" I asked.

It seemed absurd that this was her plan all along. We had nothing to go on other than the mystery person liked to steal precious jewels, and the identity of three of his targets. We didn't know if there were more targets on their list, or if it was just limited to the three. Going shop to shop would take ages and at that rate, Lucy Walker would be back in town before we made any more progress. There was no way she wouldn't notice the mud on her floor and broken glass that I was too lazy to clean up. And there would be no way for her to overlook the fact that her entire stash of jewelry was missing. Unless she came back from her trip missing her sight. But that was just way too improbable, despite everything being so crazy in my life.

"We must do whatever it takes to solve the case. Look at it like we are on a stakeout."

"A stakeout on every single person in the city?"

The walk to the chiropractic office was short, and we soon found ourselves at the front doors of the Cracking Chiropractic.

The bell above the door chimed as we made our way into the office.

"Afternoon, ladies!"

A middle-aged man greeted us as he came around a corner and into the waiting area. Mrs. Higgins leaned over to whisper hushed words in my direction. "He is new."

We were getting a lot of new people in town recently, it seemed.

"Is Doctor Charles in today?" she asked the man.

"Of course! Do you have an appointment?"

The man rushed behind the counter to tap away on the computer. He could try as hard as he wanted, but he wouldn't find us on his appointment schedule—unless Mrs. Higgins had planned on us coming here. Which was always a chance with her sixth sense.

"No, but I'm sure she won't mind seeing us."

He looked hesitantly our way as he tapped away a

bit more on the keyboard. His fingers moved rapidly before he paused once more to look at us. Then he typed some more. What was he typing? He finished up and gave us a smile before walking off.

"We should keep our eye on him. I didn't know there was a new person working here," Mrs. Higgins said as her hand came to rest under her chin. She looked at the spot the man had just occupied. No doubt she was puzzled that someone had snuck into town without her picking up on it, but she couldn't be in every place at all times. She was only human. The man returned from whatever was behind the corner, and motioned us to the small seating area.

"The doctor will be out to see you soon," he stated as he made his way back behind his desk to sit down and once again tap rapidly on the keyboard. I took in the tiny space. A two-seater couch was on one side of the room, facing the window. On the same wall as the window were two chairs with a small table in between them. I plopped myself down on the couch to wait and stared out the window, watching people pass by. I wasn't sure exactly what we were going to ask the doctor, but Mrs. Higgins would lead the way. She was the expert detective.

A shift in the couch cushion caused me to look up and see that I was joined by my partner. She had gotten her hands on a magazine and was happily flipping through it while we waited for our time to see the doctor. With nothing else to do, I went back to staring outside, or at least I attempted to. Because off in a corner of the waiting room, a movement caught my eye, and something was making its way closer to where I was seated.

My body tensed, and I could feel my palms sweat with each step it took. It closed the distance between us quickly, and I soon had a cat sitting right in front of me. It was also sitting in front of Mrs. Higgins, but she wasn't paying it any attention.

"Hello."

My eyes darted back to the window, and I tried to ignore the cat's attempt to talk to me. Don't acknowledge it and it would go away like a bad dream, I hoped.

"Hello."

The plan wasn't working. I needed to try something different.

"Do they have anything I could read?" I asked Mrs. Higgins as I turned to face her.

She briefly dipped her magazine down to show her face and told me they only seemed to carry the one ancient issue. Well, that wasn't going to help my situation.

"Why read that nonsense when you could talk to me?"

I peered down at the cat with a rusty orange coat and couldn't help but think of Rusty. The name Rusty would definitely fit this cat way more than the bright orange cat that now called the library his home.

"I know you understand me."

"Go away." I muffled the words while also attempting my best to hiss it out. I meant business, and I did not need a cat talking to me in public.

"Did you say something?"

My mouth fell open and my eyes widened at Mrs. Higgins' question. She had heard me!

"What? No!" I quickly replied.

"Weird. I thought I heard something. Must be my age getting to me."

She cracked the magazine booklet again and dove back into the words on the page. My hands were sweating profusely now. At this rate, I would create puddles from how anxious I was.

"Nice one."

Ignore the cat.

I chanted it over and over in my head. It was like counting sheep—eventually, you would fall asleep. In my case though, eventually the cat would go away. Hopefully.

"What did I do to get on your radar?" asked a soft voice.

I turned to the new voice that had joined us. A very tall woman had entered the main room. Easily over six feet tall with shoulder black hair and hazel eyes, she stuffed her hands into the pockets of her coat and leaned against the wall while taking us both in.

"Training someone?"

"Yes. this is Kat."

"I'm not being trained," I chimed in. I knew what she had meant by being trained, but I wanted nothing to do with trouble and the mysteries of the town—crimes that were increasing rapidly in number, and targeting me for some odd reason. I wanted nothing to do with that. I would rather wipe my hands clean of everything.

"Right ... so what is it today? Need some work done?"

"We have some questions, actually. Have time to sit down with us?"

Mrs. Higgins motioned to one of the empty chairs across from us, as if this was her office and not Dr. Charles' office, which it seemed the doctor picked up on, because her eyebrow raised slightly, but she made her way over to the chair.

"Michael, go restock, please." She barked out the command to the man behind the counter as she sat down. She crossed her legs, clasped her hands together, and looked at Mrs. Higgins. With the new order, Michael excused himself from the front to disappear into the back. The nameless rusty-colored cat sat beneath the doctor's chair, her eyes still focused on me. Her tail swished back and forth as she took me in, but she didn't say another word.

"He could have stayed; we aren't discussing anything top secret."

"I never know when it comes to you, April. I

remember the crazy stuff you used to come to me about back in the day."

"You act like we are old now."

"Aren't we?"

Both of the ladies laughed at the cheeky reply from Dr. Charles.

"So why are you here?"

"Well, I am sure you have heard that Delores Fuller's home was broken into."

"Yes, I also heard Lucy Walker's home was broken into."

Mrs. Higgins shot a smile my way before turning back to Dr. Charles to continue the conversation. I wasn't sure if I was supposed to be taking notes or something. I didn't want to seem eager and give people the wrong impression that I liked to solve crime. Solving crime was a habit I didn't want to develop. It was supposed to be a one-off deal, but here I was already on case two.

"I was wondering if you've heard anything about who might be the culprit?"

"Why would I have information on that? Don't you think it is best to ask that detective husband of yours?"

"He is retired, and you know I'm not supposed to be solving mysteries anymore."

"So why are you wearing expensive jewelry out in public, when there has been jewelry stolen from two people so far?"

Mrs. Higgins brought her hands up to her neck to

clutch her necklace and then played with it. She paused before replying, shifting her body to me and nodding her head. Maybe she wanted me to take over the questioning? Well, I would do my best despite not knowing what the heck to do.

"Dr. Charles, has there been anyone walking through those doors lately that seemed suspicious?"

She shifted her gaze to look in my direction as she took me in.

"Other than you two? Not really."

I nodded my head before tapping my chin, thinking of another question to follow up with. "Was there anyone who booked appointments around the time Lucy had hers?"

"Good question," whispered Mrs. Higgins in my direction.

Maybe I could be cut out for this detective stuff after all—if I ever wanted to pursue it as a career.

"I don't think you will find any information here."

My eyes drifted toward the cat, who sat calmly under Dr. Charles' chair. I did my best not to give away to the two ladies that someone else was talking to me —namely, the cat.

"Again, no one suspicious other than you two."

"And Delores?"

"Haven't seen Delores here in ages, so it's safe to say no one followed her here."

"Great. I think we have all our information. Time to head out."

I turned to Mrs. Higgins who motioned to the door. It didn't seem like we would get any other information from this place, other than Lucy came to see Dr. Charles, and Delores did not.

"I heard you are offering your services to us felines."

I wanted to correct the cat that I was indeed not offering my services and that this was some huge mistake where I kept getting pulled into things against my will. But I couldn't correct the cat in front of Mrs. Higgins and Dr. Charles. Especially not Dr. Charles. While she was a chiropractor, I was sure she could write my ticket to get me locked up in a straitjacket if she thought I could understand cats.

"I guess we're off to the next place on our list."

"Delores never came here, but I ran into her a few times at the pet shop, on the rare occasion she left her house."

"Thanks for the tip. We shall take our leave."

Mrs. Higgins stood and headed to the door to go outside. I hesitated, though, because the cat was still looking at me. I really wanted to correct the cat about its earlier statement, but Dr. Charles made no move to get out of her seat. Finally, I accepted that I would have to leave before it got too awkward and I pushed out of my seat to follow Mrs. Higgins. I only hoped that the cat didn't come to search me out later asking for a favor because my answer would be a big fat no.

Chapter Twelve

The doors of the locally owned pet shop, Pete's Supplies, slid open soundlessly. The name of the store didn't scream that it was a pet shop, but since it was the only pet shop in town, it didn't need to. It would be hard to get it confused with another.

"Why April, you are looking absolutely amazing today!"

Mrs. Higgins smiled as she made her way into the shop. She went right up to Pete, who grabbed her hand and twirled her around.

"I don't have any fancy occasions to attend with the police anymore, so I don't have anywhere to dress up. I just thought it would be fun for a change."

"That dress, collecting dust in the closet? That is a shame!" Pete let go of Mrs. Higgins' hand and turned his attention to me, his green eyes peering at me.

I took in his appearance. He had short, blond hair,

wore a floral shirt with a few buttons undone, and some boater shorts. I couldn't see his shoes, but if I had to guess, he was probably wearing some flip-flops. Pete looked more like he should be at the beach instead of working at a pet shop.

"Kat, are you here for some more supplies for the new fur babies?"

I had stopped by his shop after acquiring the cats so I could pick them up some toys. But picking up a few more wouldn't hurt, so I nodded my head. Pete came out from behind the counter and I was indeed correct that he was wearing flip-flops. He headed toward the cat section of the store.

"What do we need today? This new automatic cat litter box just came in. Super fancy and efficient!"

"Just some cat toys, most likely. Not in the market for another litter box."

Mrs. Higgins followed us as we made our way down the aisles. Pete explained every toy as we walked, letting me know what would be best for certain cats. While toys with catnip were okay, one didn't want every toy to be filled with catnip. The cats needed a variety and with three different cats, that couldn't ring truer.

"Squeakers, come here!" Pete hollered as he set a few toys on the ground. A furless and really upset-looking cat made its way over to us.

"I can't understand why he got that cat. It always

looks like it is about to kill someone." Mrs. Higgins whispered.

I thought Lola was crazy but if my friend had given me this cat to take care of, I would sleep with both eyes open every night.

"Stupid human won't let me rest in peace," the cat muttered, causing my eyes to widen as he continued to stroll toward the toys on the ground. "What does he want now?"

"Squeakers, pick a toy."

"I hate that name. Why does he call me that?" He spoke once more, obviously very displeased with the obnoxious name given to him by his owner. Nevertheless, to humor his human, he prodded the toys with his paw and finally settled on one. He bit into it, and the toy let out a loud squeak! I did my best to muffle my laughter, but it was hard since now I understood exactly how he'd gotten his name.

"Buy a few toys and take them home to see what works best for your cats."

I nodded and still tried my best to stifle my laugh as Squeakers happily played with the squeaky toy.

"Pete, we actually have some questions, and we were hoping you could help us out." Mrs. Higgins chimed in.

"Anything for you, ladies. What can I do for you?" Pete dusted his hands on his lap and stood up to face us.

Mrs. Higgins shot a look my direction, urging me to start the line of questioning.

"I'm sure you've heard about the break-in and the missing jewelry."

"Of course, who hasn't heard about it. News travels fast in this town."

"We heard that Delores Fuller frequents this shop often. Is there anyone that seems suspicious and who stops by maybe around the same time as Delores?"

Pete stood for a moment thinking, then headed to the front counter. Mrs. Higgins and I followed, leaving Squeakers with his new toy. Pete bent down behind the counter, grabbed a big leatherbound book, and dropped it on the counter. He opened the book and scrolled through the pages till he got to the last few pages and finally stopped. His finger tightly pressed to the page as he scanned it up and down, looking for whatever information he wanted to share. He flipped through a few more pages before stopping again.

"Aha! Here it is."

He looked up with a smile for Mrs. Higgins and me.

"Well, what did you find?" she asked.

"There was no one suspicious who comes in here around the time Delores comes to the pet shop. She usually has things delivered to her home, and the last time she was here was about two months ago."

"Well, that is useful information, but not exactly the information we were looking for. What else have you got in that book?"

Mrs. Higgins inched forward, trying to peer at the pages that were on display, but Pete was faster. In a second, the once-open book was now slammed closed and tucked back underneath the counter, away from Mrs. Higgins' prying eyes.

"Nothing that should be shared with someone as notorious as you."

A grin spread on Mrs. Higgins' face, and I rolled my eyes. Even though we were neighbors, the more time I spent out and about with her in a non-group setting, the more I realized there was way more to Mrs. Higgins than I had thought. I always assumed she enjoyed knowing information so it would help fuel her gossip ring and she would have lots to talk about with her friends. But it was so much more than that. She was the sleuth in the neighborhood and the volunteer neighborhood watch. She was Sherlock, and I had gotten cast as Watson, despite not having applied for the position.

"I'm starved. Back to the café, Kat, or do you want to try another spot?"

"You are the boss, so lead the way." I motioned toward the door.

We both said goodbye to Pete, and I let her walk out of the shop first but followed close behind. We made our way to the sidewalk and headed in the direction of the café.

"That was kind of a bust, don't you think?"

"I'm not really sure what we should do next to sniff

out the jewel thief. Just walking around with you wearing your diamonds doesn't seem to be doing the trick."

"Indeed. We shall rethink our plan once we arrive at the café and order some food."

The walk was short, and we arrived there in no time at all—a perk of living in a small town, where things were close together. The bell chimed once more, signaling our entry as we entered the café. The two people behind the counter looked up to greet us.

"Back already?" Daniel called out from behind the counter, as Eric smiled broadly. Mrs. Higgins strolled forward to lean against the counter and I joined her a few seconds later.

"It's a lot of work, trying to capture someone when there is no information to go off. So we took a break to get food." Mrs. Higgins exclaimed.

"Food always helps one think more clearly. Who knows, the brief break might actually help direct you in the right direction." Daniel spoke.

"That is absolutely correct! Would you make me an iced tea and a sandwich?"

"Of course, and for you, Kat?"

"Just an iced coffee is fine for me."

I gave Daniel my card, and he promptly returned it after swiping it to pay for our meals. We opted to find a table to sit at while we waited for our food to be made. Daniel soon walked out from behind the counter and headed our direction with a tray in hand. He placed it on the table and passed out our items.

"I hope you ladies don't mind if I join you for a bit?"

A small jolt of pain shot up my leg as Mrs. Higgins kicked me under the table, with a huge smile on her face as she did so. I squinted as I took in her devious smile. She had mentioned that I should go on a date with Daniel, but I didn't think she would make such fast work of trying to set things up. Nonetheless, to humor her, I nodded to Daniel, and he pulled up a chair to join us.

"So, Kat, what do you think we should do next?" Mrs. Higgins asked me.

"Maybe go to the police and see if they've found any new information?"

"We could, but that would be no fun."

Solving a crime wasn't technically supposed to be fun, I thought. The crime just needed to be solved so we all could move on with what we had been doing. While having it be fun would make it more eventful, it wasn't a requirement, by a long shot.

"You are looking into the jewelry thief, correct?" Daniel asked.

"Correct. Both Delores Fuller and Lucy Walker were targeted, but we can't seem to find anything in common between the two." Mrs. Higgins spoke.

"We went to the library, but only Delores goes there," I continued. "We went to the chiropractic office but only Lucy goes there. Finally, we went to the pet shop but only Delores goes there. Delores and Lucy don't run in the same social group, either, so it is hard to find out what they have in common."

We really did not know where to go next, and solving this case almost seemed impossible. So how did the thief know to target them? Maybe there were multiple thieves, but if that was the case, the number break-ins around town would be higher. Then there was the small matter of the person who had broken into my home. So what did Delores, Lucy, and I have in common?

Things weren't adding up again, and it was turning into a wild goose chase. The case needed to be solved before Lucy Walker got back into town, but at this rate, we would have to go to every shop to figure out if both Delores and Lucy went there. On top of that, Mrs. Higgins would need to wear her diamonds every day to help sniff out of the culprit, who had very sticky fingers.

"It just doesn't make sense. I feel like we are missing a huge clue."

"You are exactly right, Kat. Something is missing, but what, exactly?"

"The café," Daniel spoke up.

"Yes, we are at the café. That isn't missing," I countered, not understanding what he was talking about.

"No, Kat, the café is the central location."

"What do you mean?"

"Everyone comes to the café, including both Delores Fuller and Lucy Walker."

That statement got the lightbulb inside my brain shining so brightly it could have rivaled the sun. The café was the central location! Of course! One always needed food, and to get a quick bite, it was smart to go to the best café in town.

"You are so right! It has to be the café!"

"Well, Kat, looks like we know where to lay our trap for our thief."

I shot a smile in Mrs. Higgins' direction, but I focused back on Daniel, who also wore a smile, proud at having helped put the last piece of the puzzle together.

"Has anyone acting suspicious come into the café recently?"

"Honestly, I'm not sure. They keep us pretty busy here. I just know that Delores and Lucy both come here, and of course you."

I nodded in thanks. He had already provided a huge clue, and I could not expect him to solve the case for us, despite how nice that would be.

"We should stay here longer, don't you think, Kat?" Mrs. Higgins asked as she brought her hands to her earrings and played with them. Her eyes darted around the café to see if she could find anyone who might be interested in the shiny pieces of jewelry she was wearing.

"I guess that doesn't sound too bad."

Whatever helped us solve the case sounded ideal.

"Well, Daniel, why don't you tell Kat more about yourself?"

I shot a knowing look at Mrs. Higgins who tried to look innocent, but I knew better. She was one smart, tricky lady who seemed to always get her way. Daniel obliged her request by starting right into his story while I just sat with my iced coffee in hand.

Chapter Thirteen

After spending several hours—a little more than we had intended—at the café, we made our way home. Time had gone by quite fast, because Daniel turned out to be a very good storyteller and had both Mrs. Higgins and I were engrossed in every word he spoke—to the point that we had lost track of who exactly was entering and leaving the café. But surely if the thief had arrived at the café while we were present, they must certainly have noticed Mrs. Higgins? She stuck out like a sore thumb, with her extremely fancy attire and, of course, all the shine from wearing diamonds.

"Mrs. Higgins, do you think we did enough to lure the thief out?" I questioned as we walked down the street to our homes.

"Only time will tell, but I have a very good feeling that these diamonds would tempt anyone!"

I waved goodbye as I made my way up the sidewalk to my front door. But before I could put my key in the lock, she called out to me.

"What do you think you are doing?"

"Going home?"

"Absolutely not. The case continues—even at night. Grab a bag and head right over," she called out as she entered her home, leaving me on the front steps of mine, confused.

Why did I have to sleep over at her place when we were next-door neighbors? I shook my head to get rid of the confusion that always followed after hanging out with Mrs. Higgins. I entered my home where another kind of craziness waited for me in the form of talking cats.

"You have been gone a long time! Thought I was going to die from hunger!" Luna spoke.

"Stop being overdramatic. It really wasn't that long." I closed the door behind me and strolled into the kitchen to open a can of wet cat food for the very talkative cats.

"I won't be here tonight, so don't destroy the house while I am away."

"Does it look like we destroyed the house while you were gone all day?" Lola snapped in between huge bites of food.

I ignored the rude remark from the cat. I headed to my room to pack a bag for a last-minute sleepover at the neighbors'. With a few pieces of clothing and my toiletries stuffed into an overnight bag, I was all set to sleep on Mrs. Higgins' couch for the night.

"Be good! Please, please do not be destructive while I'm gone. It's just one night."

"Can't make any promises."

Against my better judgment, I left them alone at home and headed on over to the Higgins' house.

"What are you doing here?" Mr. Higgins asked as he answered the front door.

"Mrs. Higgins said I should stay the night."

"And you listened to her?" He cracked the door open wider, allowing me to enter. I already knew where I could find Mrs. Higgins, since she always drifted toward the kitchen, and that was the way I went.

"Good. I'm glad I didn't have to remind you to come over."

It didn't seem like her earlier words had been a question or an offer, more like a command that she expected me to spend the night. No ifs, ands, or buts.

"I'm making some tea, would you like a cup?"

I set my bag down on one of the empty chairs and slid into the other while nodding my head.

"What kind of action plan are we putting together that requires me to sleep over?"

"Well, think of it like a stakeout. We must always be alert now that the net has been cast."

"So we wait?"

"Exactly! A thief cannot resist their sticky fingers, especially if they think it's easy pickings."

Mrs. Higgins set two cups of tea on the table and she sat down in her usual spot. She had already changed out of her dress and put the jewels away. Now she wore a simple pajama set with her hair pulled up in a bun.

"I hope you don't mind crashing on the couch for tonight. Mr. Higgins will be heading off to bed real soon."

"No problem at all." Even though I could just go home and sleep in my own bed and walk back over early in the morning, when Mrs. Higgins offered her help to solve this case, I should take the help she offered.

"Can you explain why she can't walk the two feet to her own home and sleep there?" Mr. Higgins' voice asked from the living room, letting us know his displeasure at having someone else staying in his home.

"Because we are working on something."

"And it's related to the thefts that have been going on?"

"She just has some questions, isn't that right, Kat?"

I decided it might be best to not answer. Instead, I brought my cup of tea to my lips and slurped it down while Mr. and Mrs. Higgins continued to talk to each other from different rooms.

"Don't listen to that crazy fool. No matter what the

situation is, you are always welcome here." Her eyes darted toward the living room before she continued talking, but this time in a whisper. "Especially if we are solving a case." A huge smile appeared on her face.

"Go to bed so Kat can have the couch!"

I half-expected him to grumble and protest like before, but he headed to bed without a word.

"Let me know if you need anything to make yourself comfortable. I already set some blankets and extra pillows out for you."

With those parting words, Mrs. Higgins got up from her seat, put her cup in the sink, and made her way to her bedroom to go to sleep. With no more bickering between the Higgins, silence surrounded me.

I finished my cup of tea and placed it in the sink as well. Tonight, I would sleep on the couch instead of sleeping in my comfy bed, but it was just for one night so it wasn't a huge problem, just an odd request.

In the morning we would get back to solving the case and narrowing down the list of suspects so we could finally figure out who stole from Delores Fuller and Lucy Walker. I lay down on the couch and wrapped myself in several of the blankets set out for me. As I settled in, my eyes got heavy and soon I was off to dreamland. But just like a few nights before, a loud noise dragged me awake from my dreams.

I reached out, my fingers groping about as I tried to locate where I had last put my phone. I brought it up to my face and clicked a button on the side and a bright light made my eyes shut tightly in response. It had only been a few hours since I'd fallen asleep. Where was that noise coming from? Was the noise just a common occurrence at the Higgins home?

I set my phone back down on the table so it would be easier to find if I ended up needing it again. I wrapped myself in a blanket cocoon and attempted to go back to sleep, but the rustling noise happened again. I let out a frustrated huff as I threw the blankets off. I stared at the ceiling since it seemed sleep would evade me once more. The rustling noise stopped, only to be followed by the sound of a door creaking open.

My heart raced—the noise was way too close to the couch to be the sound of Mr. or Mrs. Higgins making a midnight kitchen run. Maybe if I didn't look, everything would go away, and it would mean it was just a bad dream and not someone trying to break in the house. I wanted to cry at my horrible luck for this was my second break-in, but then the person would know someone was on the couch and that was the last thing I wanted them to notice.

Footsteps padded through the kitchen and into the hallway. If the person went one way, they would end up in the living room and if they went the other way, they would head toward the bedroom. Which wasn't a good thing as well. I sucked in my breath and held it as I listened for what the person would do. The footsteps paused, debating which way to go, before they drifted toward the bedroom.

It was now or never.

With my hand firmly grasping my blanket and my pillow tightly clutched as well, I jumped up and lunged at the intruder. I threw the blanket over the tall figure, which looked eerily familiar to the figure of the one who had broken into my home. I covered the figure with the blanket and let loose a battle cry as I whacked them with the pillow. Not once, but several times.

The pillow wouldn't do any harm, maybe disorient the person at best, but it was just a pillow in the end. But the commotion I made was loud enough for the Higgins' bedroom door to slam open and a figure hurl toward the blanket-cloaked person, slamming them to the ground. I halted my pillow attack to glance at Mr. Higgins, who wrestled with the intruder.

"What in the world is going on? Who is under this blanket?"

"I don't know, they just broke in."

"Kat, are you okay?" Mrs. Higgins called as she too emerged from the safety of her bedroom.

"Don't just stand there! Grab something so we can tie this person up!" Mr. Higgins yelled.

Both Mrs. Higgins and I scrambled, trying to find something to help Mr. Higgins. What could help him tie the criminal up? I rushed to the kitchen, slamming the cabinets open, but nothing seemed long enough or sturdy enough to tie up a human.

"Argh!"

Panic flooded through me. I needed to find something to help Mr. Higgins before he got overpowered. I moved around the kitchen trying to find anything that could be used, and my eyes landed on the door that led to the backyard, where strung across the fence were string lights that twinkled in the night. Those could definitely tie up a human. I bolted out of the kitchen through the door to the backyard and made my way over to the lights. I firmly grasped the lights and yanked, and they came cascading down from the fence. With no time to spare, I ran back to Mr. Higgins. Adrenaline rushed through my body and the distance between us was closed quickly.

I threw the string lights on the blanket-covered body. Mr. Higgins still wrestled with the figure, so I got to work trying to tie the person up without including Mr. Higgins.

"I'm too old to be doing this anymore," Mr. Higgins gasped as he fell back on his butt and landed on the floor.

The figure underneath the blanket, who was now wrapped up in string lights, flopped about, trying to get free.

"I knew you could do it, love." Mrs. Higgins said as she reemerged from the bedroom with nothing in hand. Good thing I had been able to find something to use, or Mr. Higgins would still be wrestling away, trying to subdue the intruder.

"Craziness every day now!" He huffed as he got to

his feet and made his way over to the phone. He dialed the police to report the crime and have them come pick up the suspect. Which left Mrs. Higgins and I staring at the figure on the floor.

"Isn't this exciting?"

I rolled my eyes at Mrs. Higgins' excitement at tempting a thief to the point he had been lured to rob her home while we all slept. I crashed onto the couch. The adrenaline was leaving my body and made me want to collapse from exhaustion. What I would give to be at home in my own bed and away from all the crazy nonsense that kept unfolding in the world every day.

Chapter Fourteen

"So let me get this straight. You set a trap to lure a criminal, who had already robbed two houses, to rob you?" Detective Davidson asked.

"Not exactly," Mrs. Higgins answered.

"What exactly were you planning?"

"Well, that was to be the discussion tomorrow morning. We were going to figure out the next steps. But things kind of worked themselves out tonight."

That was a colossal understatement. I wasn't sure if Mrs. Higgins was just saying that because we really were going to plan the next steps tomorrow morning, or she was trying to play down the fact that she had tempted a thief to rob her.

"And Kat, you think this is the same person who broke into your home?"

"Same clothes and figure, so possibly," I answered as I sat up straighter on the couch. Detective Davidson took in my words and Mrs. Higgins' words before scribbling away in that notebook of his once more.

"Right, well, let's get some handcuffs on our suspect and see who we have underneath that blanket."

My eyes darted to the figure on the floor. He had long ago stopped trying to squirm his way out of his bindings of string lights. Now he just lay motionless on the ground waiting for his fate, the grand revealing of his face. Detective Davidson bent down and the sound of handcuffs tightly clasping on the prone figure's wrists echoed faintly in the room.

He helped the figure to his feet as we all gathered around with bated breaths, waiting for the reveal. The string lights that had bound our suspect untangled themselves and fell to the ground, and now it was just the blanket and handcuffs.

"Would you like to do the honors?" Detective Davidson asked me.

A lump formed in my throat. I made my way toward the figure, gently wrapped my fingers around the blanket, and tugged lightly. The blanket dropped forward a little, but not enough to show the face of the figure. I tugged on the fabric harder, throwing all caution to the wind. It wasn't like the person could do anything with handcuffs on.

"Lewis?" I whispered.

"Who is Lewis?" Mr. Higgins asked from his seated position in his favorite chair.

"The personal fitness instructor I ended up going on a date with."

"Sounds like you are free to give Daniel a call, then," Mrs. Higgins chimed in.

She was technically telling the truth—without Lewis in the picture, I could give Daniel a call, but it was too soon. And Lewis' face staring back at me was still nerve-wracking. I must really be a trouble magnet.

"We are going to take this fellow down to the station. Thanks everyone for your good work, but let's try not to do this again."

"I absolutely agree! I'm retired! You hear that, April? R-E-T-I-R-E-D!" Mr. Higgins hollered.

Mrs. Higgins paid no mind to her husband, who kept shouting from his chair. Instead, she turned toward me and shot a smile my way.

"You can head home if you want, but you are more than welcome to still stay over."

"Again, why can't she just walk the two feet to her own home?"

"Give Daniel a call since things fell through with Lewis."

With those parting words, she turned and headed toward her bedroom. Detective Davidson took that as his cue to escort Lewis out of the Higgins' home and down to the police station. Which just left Mr. Higgins and me in the living room. I could stay the night, but honestly sleeping in my bed sounded like the best thing ever. With phone and bag in hand, I waved goodbye to Mr. Higgins and headed home.

"Why are you coming home in the middle of the night?" Lola asked as I entered my house.

"Am I not allowed to come back to my home whenever I want?"

"We thought you were that intruder again," Lola responded.

"No, that happened at the Higgins home."

"Well, at least it wasn't here."

With those parting words, Lola padded off to go do whatever cats did after midnight. Knowing her, it probably revolved around creating some kind of mass chaos, like world domination.

After dropping my bag on the floor, I headed straight to my bedroom. My feet dragged and my eyes felt heavy as I fell onto my bed. The day had been a crazy mess of activity—first walking all around town, then when Lewis broke into the Higgins' home. It was just too much. Exhaustion finally took over.

Ring ... ring ...

My hand shot out from under the blanket trying to locate the absurdly loud noise that dragged me from my dreams.

"Good morning, sunshine! It is morning there, right? Sometimes I get confused." I squinted at the face that stared at me from the screen. A scowl formed at being woken up so early by my best friend.

"Why do you look like you are going to kill me? Did you wake up on the wrong side of the bed?"

"It's hard to get sleep when I had to subdue someone as they broke into a house."

"No way! Tell me all about it! I think I need to come live where you live! It sounds like you have an adventure every day!" she exclaimed excitedly. She moved closer to the camera as if it would help her see better.

"Turns out all the break-ins and jewelry thefts were because of Lewis."

"Wait, Lewis Lewis? As in, Lewis, the guy you went on a date with?"

"The one and only."

Laughter erupted from my friend and she fell back, causing the phone to drop out of her hands and slam against something, most likely the ground. Her laughter continued to ring out as she picked up the phone once more and brought it back up to her face. Her cheeks glistened with tears. She was laughing so hard she'd started to cry.

"You have some horrible luck with men!"

"Thanks for pointing that out."

"So how did he do it? Did you get the jewelry back?"

"I actually don't know. I guess I should go check in with Detective Davidson to find out what else he could glean from Lewis."

"Well, you should probably get to that, because doesn't Lucy Walker come back tomorrow?"

I stared at my friend as she spoke. I knew Lucy Walker was returning, and that it was soon, but I had forgotten exactly when she was returning. At least the case was solved with a day to spare. Hopefully, we could return the jewelry before she got back, and everything would be back to normal.

"Yeah, I should. I will call you later."

"Take care! Say hi to the cats for me!"

I looked down at my clothing; I was in my pajamas. I could technically go to the police station in those, but probably shouldn't. After heading to the closet to swap my pajamas for some comfy daytime clothes, I was ready and on my way to the front door.

"I'm heading out too. My business is done here."

Not even looking at the cat who had spoken, I popped the door open and headed outside. The feline in question followed right behind me. I closed the door behind the cat and made my way out to the street to go to the police station. The feline followed behind me.

"Why are you following me?"

"I'm not. I am heading this way."

"You have business in the city?"

"Am I not allowed to?"

"I thought you just hung out in the woods."

"I do a lot of things you don't know about."

My feet only paused for a second before I

continued on walking. Lola was definitely the weirdest cat that existed, no doubt about it.

"Oh, do you know anything about cats trying to hire me?" I asked, as I turned to face the feline behind me. Who was actually not behind me anymore. Where had she gone? I looked around, but couldn't see any traces of her. She had simply vanished.

Oh well.

The rest of the walk to the police station was quiet, and a pleasant break from all of the crazy-filled days that seemed to follow me about.

"Good morning, Kat! I heard all about your crazy adventure last night," Joe hollered from his seat behind the front desk in the police station.

"Hi Joe, is Detective Davidson in? I have some questions about what is going to happen now."

"Of course. Head on up, you know where he sits."

I nodded my thanks to Joe and scurried up the steps just in time to see Detective Davidson hang up the phone and wave me over.

"Good morning, Kat. Thanks for your help in solving the case."

"No problem. Did Lewis say anything about it?"

Detective Davidson closed his notebook and straightened the papers on his desk. He leaned back in his chair and clasped his fingers together as he stared at me.

"It was all a weird coincidence, really. He went to the gym, saw Lucy Walker there and the jewelry she wore. He then mentioned running into you, so he gave you his card. He scoped out Lucy Walker's routine, which led him to the café, where he stumbled upon Delores and also found out where they both lived. He noticed you lived across the street from Lucy, so he asked you to the café to make his activity on the block seem less suspicious."

Detective Davidson explained how Lewis had meant to rob Lucy first since she was his first target, but he couldn't pass up the opportunity of stealing from Delores. All I could really focus on was the fact that Lewis hadn't even liked me. He'd just used me in order to commit crimes under the radar. That hurt.

"Thanks for the information, detective. Any news on the jewelry?"

"The jewelry? Yeah, the pieces are long gone."

Dread settled in my stomach. The jewelry pieces couldn't be gone! Lucy Walker was returning tomorrow, and her jewelry needed to be in her home before then—and that wouldn't be possible if they were gone.

"I'm sorry. Can you say that again?"

"He already fenced the jewelry, so it's going to be extremely hard to get it back. It would be best to file with the insurance company. Which reminds me, I still haven't been able to get in contact with Lucy Walker. She does know about everything that has unfolded, right?"

"Hmm," I mumbled, refusing to construct a full sentence as it would give my dread away.

Lucy Walker, in fact, did not know what was going on.

"Right, I think it would be best for me to head home."

"Wait a moment... There was still one item he had" Detective Davidson spoke as he pulled open his desk draw and dug inside for something. I wasn't going to get my hopes high for he said the jewelry was already fenced but maybe if there was just one item left, it would appease my neighbor. He yanked out a bright pink bowl with jewels scattered across it as he held it out to me. Hesitantly, I reached out for the item and grasped within my fingers.

"What is it?" I asked.

"It's a food bowl. I'm assuming it belongs to Delores Fuller unless that is yours?" he countered.

I shook my head no, as the thief didn't manage to steal anything from home, which would have been impossible since nothing of worth was actually in my home. But a decked-out food bowl with gems on it was something I certainly didn't own.

As I examined it closer, I couldn't help but laugh as the whole reason the cat came to me in the first place was because the thief had stolen from her. And for that to be the only item left after the case was solved was just bad karma. Ever since the cats started talking it has been one bad or unlucky thing after another.

"Bye, Kat! I appreciate your help on the case," Detective Davidson said as he pulled open his notebook once more and scribbled away, which left me to walk out of the police station in a trance and make my way home.

I needed to think of a way to let my neighbor know about her missing jewelry, but right now, some sleep sounded nice. A long nap would help me think clearly, and hopefully provide some guidance on what to do next.

The walk home from the police station took less time than walking there, because of the extra pep in my step from the thought of getting back to my bed. But the dread I felt inside increased as I saw another car parked in the driveway of Lucy Walker's home.

Uh-oh.

I wasn't sure when she had arrived home, but I didn't want to be around to find out. I bolted the rest of the way to my front door and managed to get it open in record time as an ear-splitting scream pierced through the air and froze my heart. The scream was followed by another sound, and I knew I was done for.

"Kat Jones!"

Thank you for reading Himalayan Heist You can find the next book Persian Pursuit here: https://www. irisleigh.com/home/cat-aunt-cozy-mystery/

About Iris Leigh

Iris Leigh stumbled upon the genre of cozy mystery by accident. Since Iris is easily scared she does her best to avoid horror books, tv shows, and films. But dying for some type of mystery without all the suspense to make her heart burst from terror was when someone asked if she had ever read a cozy mystery. Now she has fallen in love with the genre and started to write to bring her stories to life.

If you want to stay in contact with Iris and learn about upcoming releases, make sure to sign up for the newsletter! You can sign up by navigating to her website!

Website: www.irisleigh.com

A vacant home. A new neighbor. A desperate cat. A one-time job.

I'm Kat Jones, and no matter what anyone tells you, I don't work for cats… unless it's the only option.

The vacant home in my neighborhood has been vandalized. But that's not the worst of it. If the new neighbors don't move in, the cat they adopted has to go back to the shelter. I can't let that happen.

Someone is out to get them. It's my job to find out who and why. Then, that's the last time I let myself get hired by cats.

Order here! **https://www.irisleigh.com/home/cat-aunt-cozy-mystery/**